The Ghost
They Left
Behind

The Ghost They Left Behind

Susan Wallace

Matador
9 Priory Business Park,
Wistow Road, Kibworth Beauchamp,
Leicestershire. LE8 0RX
Tel: 0116 279 2299
Email: books@troubador.co.uk
Web: www.troubador.co.uk/matador
Twitter: @matadorbooks

ISBN 978 1800462 991

British Library Cataloguing in Publication Data.
A catalogue record for this book is available from the British Library.

Printed and bound in Great Britain by 4edge Limited
Typeset in 12pt Minion Pro by Troubador Publishing Ltd, Leicester, UK

Matador is an imprint of Troubador Publishing Ltd

Illustrations by Michael J Wallace

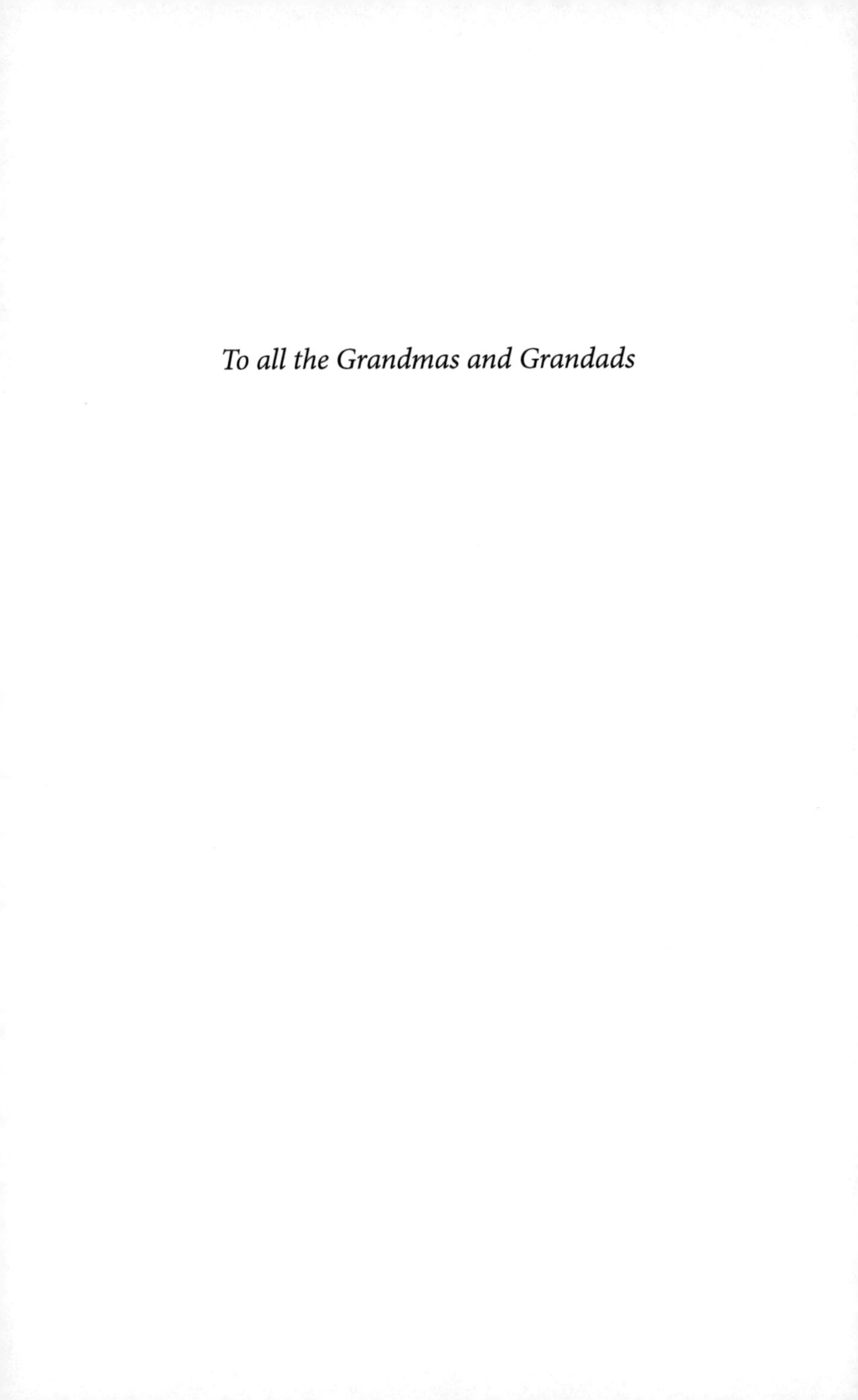

To all the Grandmas and Grandads

Preface

This story happened a long time ago. The children in it are grown up now, with children of their own. Their mum and dad are white-haired and wrinkly, and the grandparents in the story – well, they've finished all their adventures and enjoyed their lives, and gone.

It was all so long ago, in fact, that there were no mobile phones, no internet, no sat nav or email, and certainly no cool electronic devices for children to play with on long journeys. There weren't even any seat belts in the back of cars. Shocking, I know!

So now I expect you're wondering how everyone managed without all those things. Well, you'll just have to read on and see.

The ghost shook his head. "You're just a kid," he said sadly. Page 52.

chapter one

*In which we meet Tom
and Tom meets someone else.*

He was sitting on the edge of the crumbling wind-swept wall when Tom first saw him, and tugging his short skirt down to try to warm his grubby knees. A red woollen cloak hung raggedly from his shoulders. It was obviously not as long as it should have been. It looked, in fact, as though something had tried to chew it off somewhere above the knee.

What caught Tom's interest, though, was the short sword that hung from the man's belt. It was the only thing about him that wasn't shabby; and Tom, although he knew he shouldn't speak to strangers, wondered whether there was just a chance he might be allowed to hold it.

He moved a little nearer and coughed politely. The man gave no sign of having seen him. Indeed, he seemed to take no notice of anything at all: not the crowds of tourists roaming over the ruined Roman camp; not even the shrieking children who chased about the grass and leaped on and off the low remains of walls. He was simply staring miserably at the ground in front of him, every now and again sighing a huge sigh that would have misted up a window.

Tom had already decided this man must be one of those people who are paid to dress up and act a part to make the ruins more interesting. Although at this important fort on Hadrian's Wall it seemed a bit mean and stingy to have just one Roman soldier.

He certainly looked the part though, with his craggy face and bent nose. He had big muscles, too, and hairy legs which Tom thought looked a bit silly with a short skirt. In fact, Tom thought the man must be feeling a bit of an idiot altogether and that was probably why he was so glum and wouldn't look at anybody. He was most likely sulking because he didn't like the job. If Tom had to do this job, sitting about in the cold, *he* would sulk. Except for the sword. It would be cool to have the sword.

Tom coughed again and held out his crisp packet. The man ignored him. Worse. It was as though the man didn't even know he was there. Tom wrinkled his nose. From this close it was clear that as well as not being a very cheerful soul the man wasn't too clean either. His hair was greasy and lank, his neck looked a bit grey and his fingernails were black with muck. But the hilt of his sword looked bright and polished and Tom decided that as there were so many people about, shoving past them all the time, it would be ok to engage the man in conversation. So, "Excuse me!" he said loudly. "Would you like a crisp?" And he rattled the bag right under the man's nose.

Slowly the man straightened his back and turned his head to look at Tom. His brown hawk eyes seemed to stare straight through him. Tom smiled politely. "I'm sorry if I'm disturbing you," he said. "But I just wondered if you'd like a…Hey! Watch out!" The man had suddenly raised both hands and was waving them in front of Tom's face.

Tom stepped back and looked around. No-one was taking any notice. A horrible thought had struck him: what if this man wasn't paid to dress up? What if he was someone who was very disturbed and thought he really *was* a Roman soldier? And now Tom came to think about it, it wasn't that the man was ignoring all the people who were milling about; it was that all the people were ignoring *him*. And that was what you were supposed to do with people who were a bit disturbed, wasn't it? He'd seen how everyone always ignored that woman who talked to herself at the bus stop.

So, still smiling nervously, Tom began to back away. But now the man jumped to his feet, still waving his arms about. "You can see me!" he shouted; and his voice sounded harsh and rough and used to the open air. "You can, can't you?! You really can see me!"

"Er, yes," said Tom, looking around wildly. But no-one was taking any notice. And then suddenly the backs of his legs came up with a bump against the ruined wall of the camp latrine and he tried to catch his balance to stop himself from tumbling backwards into the deep trench where all the Romans' poo used to go. The soldier took a step forward and reached out a hand to steady him. And then he suddenly drew it back as though stung and stared at it, front and back, as if he thought Tom's jumper might have left a mark. Then he stared at Tom again and slowly his craggy face lit up with a grin. "By Jove! You really can see me, can't you!" he said. "And I frightened you there for a minute, didn't I? Well, I'm sorry about that." He didn't look sorry. He thumped himself proudly on the chest. "But I'm a fierce fighting man, me. And I always strike terror into people what see me."

He spoke with an accent that was only partly local Geordie, as though he'd lived here a long time but had started out somewhere else. Tom decided to play along with him. After all, there were too many people about for him to be in any danger. So he sat down on the wall and the soldier sat down beside him, still looking delighted and rubbing his big, grubby hands together.

"Have you been doing this sort of thing long?" Tom asked pleasantly.

The man's face at once fell gloomy again and he turned away, shooting Tom a sidelong look. "Long? Huh!" He gave a hollow laugh. "Only about a thousand years. Probably more like two thousand. I don't know. You lose all track of time after a while."

Tom shivered, and not just because of the chilly breeze. What if the man wasn't mad, or an actor? What if…

But that was nonsense. Tom looked up at the crowds of people wandering about the ruins in the sunshine, muffled up in their anoraks and hoodies and cagouls against the wind that blew, even in summer, from the cold north.

"I remember when someone last saw me," the soldier was saying. "Hundreds of years ago it must have been." He scratched his chin thoughtfully. "He was up here while the sun went down. Breaking up part of the barracks wall, he was. Ready to cart the stones away. Building himself a house somewhere, prob'ly. You should've seen his face when he spotted me. Hah!" The soldier threw back his head and roared with laughter. "Never seen no-one run so fast, like. Not even Picts! Nearly wet himself! Hah!" Then he stopped abruptly and fixed Tom with his hawk-like stare. "How come *you* can see me, anyway? What's your game?"

It seemed to Tom that the man was taking this acting thing much too seriously. "Why do you do this job?" he asked him. "You don't seem to be enjoying it very much."

"Listen, mate," scowled the soldier, "I'll ask the questions, right?" His eyes narrowed with suspicion. "Like, what was that thing you was rattling under my nose? A charm, was it? Something to get rid of me? Pouf! Like that? Gone into thin air, like?" He pushed his fierce face close to Tom's. "Well I wish you could, mate," he said bitterly. "I'm sick to the back teeth of all this." And he waved a hand at the grey ruins, the trodden grass, the crowds with their hoods up, and the hills fading into the misty distance. "Draughty pigging dump! Snow-winds howling all the winter. Idiots tramping all over it in summer. Used to be just me and the sheep. And before that…" He shook his head and turned away, his sandaled feet scuffing at the sparse grass.

Tom felt embarrassed. The crisp packet had flown out of his hand and dropped down into the latrine trench when he almost went over himself. He glanced down at it over his shoulder, and then scanned the grey and green ruins to see whether any of his family were in sight. He thought he saw his little sister, Bella, in her red dungarees, waving a guidebook about at the top of the hill. But he couldn't see Grandad, Grandma or Auntie Eileen anywhere. With their hoods up, everyone looked like everyone else.

"They were only crisps," he said. He decided not to mention that he'd hoped to have a go with the sword. The soldier was behaving so oddly that it seemed best not to remind him that he was carrying a dangerous weapon. "I thought you might be hungry," he added. The soldier didn't look at him, but gave a scornful snort. "I'm on holiday, actually," Tom went on. "Me and Bella. We're going abroad with Grandma and Grandad. They've got a new caravan and we've been staying near here just for the weekend to try it out – see if we all fit in it alright – because Auntie Eileen's coming as well. That's Grandma's sister. We're going to see how well it tows and whether the cooker works and everything. It's good fun," he added lamely, because it looked as though the soldier wasn't listening to him at all. He was just staring at the ground again, looking as gloomy as ever.

"Right. Well," said Tom. "I'd better be going I suppose. Better go and see if I can find the others before they get arrested for not looking after me properly." He stood up and glanced again regretfully at the sword. "It was nice to meet you," he said politely, and added to himself silently, *Except it wasn't!*

"That's right!" moaned the soldier. "That's right! Go on! Clear off! Leave me all on my own again. I'll just sit here for another thousand years until somebody else sees me. Thanks a lot!"

"Hey. Come off it," said Tom, who felt a bit braver now that he'd edged further away. "You don't have to keep on about that being lonely stuff. If you're supposed to be acting like a Roman soldier, you ought to march up and down a bit, do some drill, that sort of thing. That's what people like to see."

The soldier stood up suddenly, looking half hurt, half furious. "See?" he shouted. "SEE?" Tom looked around nervously, but no-one was taking any notice. "Are you stupid?" yelled the soldier. "They wouldn't pigging see *me* whatever I did! Look!" And he stamped up to an old woman in a plastic raincoat who was peering through her spectacles at a guidebook, turning it this way and that with a frown. The soldier stopped directly in front of her, put his thumbs in his ears, wiggled his fingers, stuck out his tongue and blew a loud farty noise.

The old woman took no notice at all. She adjusted her spectacles and calmly turned the page of her book. The soldier began marching on the spot, his broad chest less than a meter away from the woman's face. His knees seemed to graze her as they rose and fell. Even when, to Tom's delight, he drew his sword and

gave a wild whoop which echoed between the hills like an animal's cry, the woman gave no sign that she had seen or heard him. After a moment she turned and wandered away.

The soldier sat back heavily on the wall, breathing hard. "Ok?" he growled. "That prove it to you?"

Now, Tom found all this very hard to believe; and he might have walked away even then without completely believing it if Grandad had not come up behind him and tapped him on the head with a guidebook and said sternly, "Mustn't wander off like that, must we, eh? Get lost if we do, you know. Now don't stand there talking to yourself and staring at old ladies. People'll think you're potty. Don't want that now, do we?"

Tom cleared his throat nervously, "I was talking to him, actually," he said, pointing directly at the Roman soldier, who now stood unaccountably at attention by the wall.

Grandad looked in the direction he was pointing, frowned, and then said cheerfully, "Talking to the wall, eh? Har! Har! I've heard that walls have ears, but that's taking it a bit far. Har! Har!" And he turned away and strode down the slope, calling back over his shoulder, "Come on, Tommy Tucker. Mustn't be late. Got to get the caravan packed up, you know."

Tom turned slowly to the soldier, stared at him for a moment – the tattered cloak, the grubby knees, the big, miserable face – and then said quietly, so that no-one would notice him talking to himself, "So. You must be a ghost, then, I suppose."

"Scared now, are you?" the ghost asked slyly.

"No," lied Tom. And then he said, "You must be very lonely. Why aren't there more of you?"

The ghost began to hint darkly about some dirty deeds he had done which accounted for his present state. But he wouldn't give any details, and Tom decided he'd probably rather not know. "But do you have to stay here?" he asked. "I mean, couldn't you travel a bit? Look for other ghosts to make friends with, that sort of thing?"

"I know this place, though, mate, you see," said the ghost. "It's pigging miserable, but at least I know it. The only other place I know is me home, and I know I'll never get back there."

"Where *is* your home?" asked Tom.

The ghost gave him a withering look. "Where do you think? Rome, of course!"

"But you don't speak Latin."

"Well, there'd not be much point, would there? You wouldn't understand what I was saying, would you?" The ghost sighed. "I still dream about it, you know. Ah, Roma!" He closed his eyes and tipped back his head. "The vines, the wine, the sun! All the year blue skies. And when the wind blows it blows warm. Not like this place. Ugh!" He spat. "It drives the cold into your bones. Mine are over there, by the way." He nodded towards the grassy slope beyond the wall.

But Tom was barely listening. He was jumping up and down with excitement, tugging at the ghost's short ragged sleeve. "Hey! Guess what! Listen! We're going to Rome. Rome is exactly where we're going. Next week. We're crossing the channel to Ostend and driving through Belgium, Germany, Switzerland and into Italy, right down to Rome."

"Then you're in luck," said the ghost gloomily. "And I'll be on my own again."

"But look," insisted Tom, "you can come with us. You've just proved other people can't see you, so you can travel with the luggage in the caravan. It's simple. No-one need even know you're there."

The ghost stared at him suspiciously for a moment and then looked away. "I don't know," he said. "Anyway, what's this *caravan* you keep on about? A bunch of camels?"

"It's like a little house on wheels," said Tom. "We pull it behind the car."

"Oh yes. *Car*. I've seen those down there." The ghost gestured towards the car park about half a kilometre away, where the rows of cars were lined up like toys with the cold sunshine glinting on their windscreens. "They've got smaller and shinier, they have, since they stopped having horses pulling 'em."

"Well, come on, then," coaxed Tom. The idea of taking a ghost on holiday with him was so exciting he just had to make it happen. "Come on, let's go."

"Just hang on a minute," said the ghost, holding up a hand and assuming that familiar expression of mistrust and cunning. "I don't want to be led into no traps."

"For goodness sake!" shouted Tom angrily, no longer caring that people were staring at him. "What else could possibly happen to you? You're dead!"

The ghost thought for a minute. Then, "True," he said, and nodded. And with a last brief glance round at the ruined camp, he followed Tom through the crowds and down the hill.

chapter two

*In which the ghost has a nasty experience
and the caravan gets a name.*

When Tom got to the car, he found all the others already sitting in it, waiting for him; Grandma and Grandad in the front and Bella in the back with Auntie Eileen.

"Come on! Come on, Tommy Tucker!" barked Grandad. From the corner of his eye Tom noticed the Roman soldier spring quickly to attention again. He pulled the car door open and jerked his head at the ghost. "Get in!" he hissed.

But the ghost hung back, eyeing the car nervously and twisting his hands together in an agitated way. The family were giving Tom some strange looks. Grandma lowered her window. "Don't stand there talking to yourself and jerking your head about, boy," she boomed. "Get in the car. We're waiting to go."

"Yes, come on, duckbods," said Auntie Eileen sweetly, reaching out from the back seat and taking hold of Tom's arm. "Come and snuggle up to me and I'll give you a nice sweetie." And Tom, as he was hauled inside, shouted urgently at the ghost, "Get in, for goodness sake! Or you'll be left behind!"

Grandma turned around in her seat and stared at him. "I've just *told* you that," she said indignantly. "What are you saying it again for? What are you giving yourself orders for? Especially when you're already *in* the car. Doesn't make sense. Gets that from *you*," she added, turning to Grandad. Tom watched Grandad's face in the rear-view mirror. He looked a bit hurt.

"Hurry up," whispered Tom, very anxious now in case the ghost might change his mind. But to his great relief at the very last minute the soldier made a desperate lunge and tumbled onto the back seat just as Auntie Eileen reached past Tom and pulled the door shut with a slam.

He was a very bristly and uncomfortable person to be squeezed up close to. His bits of metal and leather armour stuck out all over the place and felt very different from the softness of Auntie Eileen who was squashed up on Tom's other side. Tom also noticed, now that he was in an enclosed space, that the soldier didn't smell particularly nice either. It surprised him that a ghost should have any smell at all. But then if he could see him and hear him and feel him, he supposed it would be rather odd if he couldn't smell him too – although he couldn't help wishing he couldn't.

"Does someone need the toilet?" demanded Grandma.

Grandad started up the car and began to edge slowly out of the carpark. "Move up a bit, Tom," ordered Bella. "I'm all squashed and you've got miles of room. Look."

It was true that poor Bella was scrunched up between Auntie Eileen and the car door. And Auntie Eileen (who never grumbled) was squashed between Tom and Bella like a piece of cheese in a sandwich; while on the other side of Tom, invisible to all the rest, the soldier took up nearly half the back seat. Tom sighed, clambered over and sat himself between the soldier's grubby knees. Auntie Eileen and Bella shuffled along a bit.

"Jolly good," said Grandad. "Everybody comfortable?"

They were. But not for long. Tom became aware that the soldier was craning forward, peering over Grandad's shoulder. He seemed to be looking for something on the floor at the front of the car.

"You're squashing me," hissed Tom.

"Oh, I'm sorry, duckbods," said Auntie Eileen, "Let me find you some mint rock." She began fishing in her handbag.

"What are you looking for?" Tom asked the ghost irritably. He was being pressed forward into the back of Grandma's seat and felt he would soon be flat as a shirt on an ironing board.

"Just my mint rock, darling," said Auntie Eileen. "Why don't you sit back a bit? You look ever so uncomfortable."

"Yes, do sit *back*, Thomas," snapped Grandma. "You'll soon be sitting on my neck."

"The holes," said the ghost gruffly, still craning forward. "I can't see the holes. Are they under his seat or what?"

"What are you talking about?" mumbled Tom with some difficulty, his mouth squashed up against the back of Grandma's seat.

"You can't fool me, mate," said the ghost. "I know how he makes this car move along. There's nothing magic about it. He just puts his feet through the floor and runs. What gets me, though, is I can't see the holes what he puts his feet through."

"No holes," muttered Tom indistinctly. "There's an engine in the front."

"What? How? An engine of war?"

"No. An internal combustion engine."

Baffled into silence, the ghost sank back in the seat. The countryside slipped by slowly as Grandad drove along at a dawdle, singing cheerfully:

"O-oh, Bella Bella Bella!
Oh, dee dee dee dee dee!"

This song annoyed Bella very much, but she wasn't going to let Grandad know that. She sat staring crossly out the window on her side of the car, her cheeks very pink.

Grandma interrupted the singing. "Get your foot down, Grandad, for goodness sake. We'll never get home at this rate."

The ghost nudged Tom in the back. "See!" he said triumphantly. "I was right!"

As Grandad accelerated, the scenery began to flash by faster and faster. The hedges became a blur, the startled cows no sooner appearing than left behind, and Grandad broke into song again, even louder than before:

"O-oh, Bella Bella Bella!
O-oh ..."

Tom twisted round between the Roman's big grimy knees to see if he was enjoying the ride, and was alarmed to find that the ghost was cowering back on the seat with his eyes tight shut and an expression of absolute terror on his face. It had never occurred to Tom before that ghosts might turn pale, but this one had. And his fingers were gripping the edge of the seat either side of his knees until his ghostly knuckles showed white.

Tom patted the muscly arm reassuringly. "Don't you worry," he said. "It's perfectly safe. If you think this is fast, you want to wait until Grandma drives."

"I heard that," snapped Grandma. "Don't listen to him, Eileen. I never exceed the speed limit, do I, Grandad?"

Grandad said nothing.

"And anyway," said Grandma, sniffing suspiciously, "there's still a most peculiar smell in this car. Have you washed your feet lately, Grandad?"

It was just as well, thought Tom, that the ghost was too frozen by fear to notice these rude remarks. And now he'd begun to tremble, too, and Tom, trapped between his knees, found himself being shaken about like a strawberry milkshake.

"Sit still, Tom," snapped Bella. "You're making the whole seat wobble."

"I c-can't help it," said Tom. "It's the c-car b-bumping me ab-bout."

"Well, be careful you don't choke on your mint rock, duckbods," said Auntie Eileen. "Do you think you'd be more comfy if you swapped places with me?"

Tom, who could not imagine Auntie Eileen sitting on the Roman soldier's knee, politely refused and continued to be rattled up and down.

"Do you need the toilet, Thomas?" demanded Grandma.

But now, at last, they were pulling in through the gates of the field where the caravan was parked. "Here we are, then," announced Grandad. "Back at field H.Q. Time to break camp and head for home, eh?" He switched off the engine, leaned back in his seat and took a deep breath. "Er, I think I'll go off to the old washroom first, though," he said. "Throw some of the old talc about." And he got quickly out of the car.

Bella, Grandma and Auntie Eileen disappeared into the caravan, casting some curious looks back at Tom who was still wrestling about on the back seat, apparently deep in conversation with himself. In fact, he was trying his best to persuade the soldier that it was safe to open his eyes and get out of the car. When shaking and nudging wouldn't move him, Tom put his mouth close to the ghost's ear and bellowed: "OPEN YOUR EYES, YOU IDIOT! WE'VE STOPPED!"

Bella's face appeared at the caravan window. She stared at Tom for a moment, then turned to the others inside, pointed towards Tom and tapped the side of her head.

Tom felt cross and embarrassed. He clambered over the ghost and began to get out of the car. "Right, then. I'm not going to keep making myself look stupid," he muttered, "just because you're a big scare-baby."

It was a pity he hadn't said this before, because it affected the ghost like an electric jolt. His eyes shot open, he sprang forward and he grabbed hold of Tom's arm. "Who you calling scared?" he growled.

"You," squeaked Tom. "You were scared stiff."

"Pah!" said the ghost scornfully, letting go and straightening his tunic. "Rubbish! Me scared? Me? What's fought the hordes of barb'rous Picts? Never! Besides, I've rode in chariots what's gone twice as fast as that!"

Tom was shocked. He'd never heard such an outrageous lie and he didn't see why the Roman should get away with it, ghost or not. "If you weren't scared," he said sternly, "why were you sitting there with your eyes shut?"

"Obvious, innit?" snapped the ghost. "I was asleep, wasn't I? I was so bored with going fast I just fell asleep. OK?"

Tom gave a snort of disgust and got out of the car. He was already beginning to regret having invited the ghost along, and was wondering how he was going to put up with his company all the way to Rome. Could he just boot him out now and leave him behind? That would be a bit mean, he supposed. "Worse luck," he muttered to himself. And then, "Come on," he said to the ghost wearily. "You can't stay in there. We're packing up to go home. You'd better travel in the caravan when we set off again. Just keep out of the way until we're ready to go, right?"

At this moment Grandad passed them on his way back from the shower block. "Still talking to yourself, Tom?" he called cheerily. "Jolly good." And then, more quietly, but not quite quietly enough, "Strange boy."

Meanwhile, the soldier had scrambled from the car and snapped to attention with his fist clenched and his arm across his chest in a Roman salute. He remained like that, staring straight ahead of him, until Grandad had disappeared into the caravan. Then he relaxed with a sigh.

I must ask him some time why he does that, thought Tom. But he was too fed up with the ghost's silly behaviour to start another conversation just now. "You stay out here and keep out of trouble," he said instead. "I'm going to help pack up."

Inside the caravan they were all drinking tea. "Here he comes," beamed Grandad. "Got tired of talking to himself. Come to talk to us instead." He patted the seat beside him and Tom sat down.

"As long as he doesn't sit next to me," said Bella. "He's being really weird."

Now, Tom's head was full of worry and excitement about the ghost and so, before he could stop himself, he heard himself saying, "I know. But I think he's just a big show-off really." Then he stopped, just in time, before he said more. They were all looking at him with puzzled faces. He stared back at them, and then gave a loud pretend laugh. "Me, I mean," he said. "Me. I mean I'm just showing off."

Auntie Eileen came to the rescue. "No, you're not, duckbod. You're lovely." She reached across and ruffled Tom's hair. "And I know what you'd like. You'd like some treacle toffee. Come on. Here it is. It's lovely. Open wide. That's it." She thrust a big sticky chunk of toffee into Tom's mouth, and that certainly stopped him talking to himself – or to anyone else – for quite some time.

As he sat there with his cheeks bulging, Grandma leaned across the table and said sternly, "Auntie Eileen wants all your teeth to fall out."

"Oh, I don't, duckbod," said Auntie Eileen, clearly upset.

"Then stop stuffing him with sweets," snapped Grandma, and got up to wash the mugs.

There was silence for a moment, broken only by the sucking, gurgling noises coming from Tom. Then Grandad clapped his hands and announced that he thought it had been a very successful trial run for the holiday, and that all that remained now was to choose a name for the caravan before its first proper journey abroad.

"What about *HMS Sardine Tin*?" suggested Grandma, splashing about at the sink.

"*Gypsy Belle* would be the best name," said Bella firmly.

"Well," said Auntie Eileen, "I like the name Ron and I had for our first house. What about that? *Dunroamin*."

Tom's mouth was still full of toffee, so he couldn't make his own suggestion, which was *Road Monster*. But he did manage to gurgle his agreement with the others that *Dunroamin* was a pretty silly name for a caravan.

"What about *Rover*?" suggested Grandad.

"*Rover*'s a dog's name," said Bella scornfully. And so finally, to Tom's disgust, they voted Bella's suggestion of *Gypsy Belle* the best.

When everything was packed up and the van was hitched to the back of the car and Tom had managed to swallow his toffee, he went to fetch the ghost, who was sitting a little way away under a tree. He was looking lost and miserable, and Tom was suddenly quite sorry for him.

But he wasn't going to show it. "Time to go," he said breezily, a bit like Grandad would. "Are you ready?"

The ghost nodded and clambered to his feet, his leather armour creaking. "Just don't you forget, mate," he said, as Tom bundled him into the caravan. "I'm not afraid of nothing." He laid himself flat on the floor between the airbeds and buckets, and closed his eyes tightly and covered his face with his hands. "Nothing," he muttered again as Tom closed the door of the Gypsy Belle.

As they set off and Grandad broke into song again, Bella leaned across Auntie Eileen – who always had to sit in the middle to stop the children quarrelling – and whispered, "What are you up to, Tom? I know you're up to something." And Tom decided that when they got home, he had better tell her, because when Bella wanted to know something, she always found out in the end.

chapter three

*In which the ghost tells
a tale as tall as himself.*

It was late and quite dark by the time they got home. Tom had some difficulty smuggling the ghost out of the caravan before Grandma and Grandad set off again. They had to drop Auntie Eileen off at her house before they went back to their own. While Tom stood there trying to explain his reasons for opening the caravan door, he was thinking how useful it would be if this ghost could learn the trick of walking through walls.

Mum and Dad were waiting at the front door. "They've been very good," Grandad called to them. "Looking forward to Saturday. Only three days to wait, y'know. We'll pick them up early. Then it's Rome here we come." And he winked at Tom, waved goodbye, and with a roar and a rattle the Gypsy Belle pulled away and disappeared around the corner.

The soldier stood in the hall, staring about him at the electric lights, the carpets and the big old clock on the wall. He was trying to look bored, but Tom could see that he was really impressed. Bella wasn't. She was used to it. She yawned a huge yawn.

"Straight to bed," said Mum. "You can tell us all about it in the morning." Dad flipped the switch to turn on the landing light, and the ghost's head jerked round in amazement. He stared from the light to Dad, then back at the light again. "Come on," Tom whispered, tugging at him. "We're going upstairs."

"Just ignore him," Bella called down to Mum and Dad. "He's been talking to himself all day." Tom scowled at her and she stuck her tongue out at him. But they were both too tired to really fall out.

The ghost squeezed into the bathroom with them and stared around at the shiny chrome taps and the mirror tiles gradually steaming up as the hot water ran.

"Smart, isn't it?" said Tom. Bella ignored him.

"Not bad," said the ghost grudgingly. "You're rich, huh?"

Tom was cleaning his teeth. He shook his head.

"Yeah, well," said the ghost, "I could've had all this if I'd wanted. But I like the tough life. I like a bit of action, me."

He followed Tom into the toilet. There wasn't a lot of room. "It's not very friendly, this, is it?" he said disapprovingly. "You ought to have a few more seats in here. Then you could sit and talk to each other while you do your business, like what we used to do."

Tom pictured the ruined latrine back at the Roman camp and thought he wouldn't care for that arrangement very much. "This house isn't big enough," he said. He was tired and didn't want to argue.

Bella hammered impatiently on the door. "It's bad enough you talking to yourself all the time," she called, "without you locking yourself in the lavatory to do it."

Tom pushed his way past her, pulling the ghost along with him. In the bedroom the children's beds were side by side under the window. It seemed very spacious after being cramped up in the caravan for two nights. "I'm going to sleep now," Tom whispered sternly, climbing into bed. "I don't know whether you sleep or not, but you better not go wandering around in the night. You might scare someone."

The ghost grinned and his spectral teeth gleamed in the darkness. Tom felt uneasy. "Listen. If you make any trouble," he warned, "I shan't be able to take you with us to Rome, and then what will you do?"

"OK, OK," said the ghost sullenly. "I'll sleep down here." And he slumped down on the floor in the corner by the wardrobe.

When Tom woke up the next morning it was very early. At first, he thought he was still in the caravan, but then he recognised his bedroom and, with a sinking feeling in his stomach, he remembered the ghost. And there he was, still slumped on the floor by the wardrobe. But he wasn't asleep. His eyes were open and he was looking straight back at Tom.

"G'morning," mumbled Tom sleepily, and pulled his covers back up to his chin.

"Good morning," said Bella brightly from the other bed, propping herself up on one elbow. "What time is it?"

Time, thought Tom, *to tell her about the ghost.* Otherwise she'd carry on thinking he was potty for talking to himself all the time. "Listen, Bella," he said, trying to use a sensible voice like Mum's. "I want to ask you something. See over there?" He pointed at the ghost. "There by the wardrobe? Now tell me if you can see anything unusual."

"Why?" Bella was always a bit suspicious of Tom's tricks, and she couldn't think why he was suddenly talking in such a soft posh voice.

"Go on," Tom urged. "Just look."

Bella looked, then shook her head.

"No," he said. "Look *hard*."

She screwed her face up and stared into the corner. Tom could see the ghost staring back at her rudely.

"Nope," she said. "What is it? A spider? I don't care if it is. It's you who's scared of spiders, not me."

"You must be able to see something," pleaded Tom. His sister eyed him suspiciously, then looked again.

"Hmm," she said. "The only thing…it looks as though the air over there is a bit…a bit thicker. Like looking through water. It's weird. What have you done? I'm telling Mum."

The ghost was looking scornful. "She won't be able to see me," he sneered. "So you're wasting your time."

"Listen, Bella," said Tom firmly. "When we were at Hadrian's Wall yesterday, I met somebody – somebody very rude and bad tempered" – (he glared at the ghost) – "but I felt sorry for him and I said we'd take him with us to Rome because that's where he's from."

"You didn't!" said Bella, horrified.

"I did. And he's sitting in that corner now. And the reason you can't see him is because…" Tom took a deep breath, "…because he's a ghost."

"You big fibber!"

"No. Honestly. But you don't need to be scared. He won't hurt us. He wouldn't get back to Rome if he did." Tom gave the ghost another stern look.

Bella was still staring into the corner. She knew all Tom's tricks. But somehow, especially when he was telling her something scary, she couldn't help believing him.

"You know how you were going on about me talking to myself yesterday?" Tom went on. "Well, I wasn't. I was talking to him. And now that you know he's there, surely you can see him, just a bit."

Bella pulled her covers around her and shivered. She could see *something*, certainly. Now it was as though there was a sheet of glass across the corner of the room and on it, like a reflection in a shop window, was the shadowy outline of a strangely dressed, moody-looking man with a big nose. But if she looked through it, she could still see the bottom of the wardrobe, the section of skirting board and the dust at the edge of the carpet.

"Yes," she said eventually in a little voice, burrowing further down the bed so that only her eyes showed above the sheet, wide with alarm. "Is he wearing a red cloak? And does his hair need washing?"

"That's him!" shouted Tom jubilantly.

"I can see right through him, though," Bella whispered. (Bella was always very good at seeing right through people.)

"P'raps when you're used to him, you'll see him prop'ly," said Tom. "I saw him prop'ly straight away. I wonder if you can hear him as well."

Taking the hint, the ghost gave a blood-curdling wail, and then roared with laughter as Bella dived in panic right under the covers. When Tom joined in the laughter, Bella emerged and glared at them both.

"Very clever," she said crossly. "Frightening little girls. That's what *bullies* do."

"Yes," said Tom to the ghost, as though he, himself, hadn't been laughing too. "That was mean. You ought to apologise."

The Roman gave Bella curt nod. "Sorry," he said grudgingly. Bella, who could see him more clearly now, nodded back and said politely, "That's alright. Don't mention it."

"Good," said Tom. "That's better. Now," – he glanced at his Superman watch – "it's still only seven o'clock and Dad won't be making a cup of tea until about eight. So why don't you tell us some more about yourself? All your battles and stuff."

"Yes," said Bella. "That would be quite useful for school."

Somehow, Tom doubted that very much, but he nodded just the same. "Come on, then," he urged the ghost. "Tell us."

"Right," said the ghost. "I don't mind if I do. I think you'll be impressed. And scared. And surprised. And amazed…"

"Oh, just get on with it," said Bella.
And so he did.

The Ghost's Tale

Anyway (he said), *it starts off in Rome. There I was, standing in the market place, minding my own business when who should come by but the Emperor himself, carried in his chair by four strapping slaves. "Who's that tough-looking young bloke over there?" he says, pointing at me. "I want him in my army straight away. Send him off to Britannia. He's just the bloke to sort out them Picts." So I up and enlisted and they was dead pleased when they saw me in action. Marching, fighting with a sword, chucking spears – all came natural to me.*

So we marched up through Germania (Here he paused for a moment, staring in front of him as though he saw something they couldn't. Then he shook his head slightly and carried on.) *Anyway, when we was finally waiting on the coast of Gaul, ready to board the ship to Britannia, my Centurian points across to the British coast, all misty and white in the distance. "See that, lads?" he says. "They say that's the land of the dead. But we'll liven 'em up alright, eh, lads?"*

Anyway, we set sail. And it was dead calm.

Like a pond it was. Until we were about halfway across. Then suddenly, with no warning, this pigging great wave comes washing towards us – sets the ship climbing up and up and then – whoosh! – down into the trough, and then up, up, up again. And they was all panicking: oarsmen, crew, even us military. Even our Centurian. Being seasick all over the place. Slipping about. Didn't know what it was, see? But I knew.

So I goes up to the Centurian, sliding about like, because of the sick everywhere and the ship being shaken to bits, and I says, "Begging your pardon, sir, but I think you'll find the trouble what we've got here is on account of there's a sea serpent."

But it wasn't no use. He was in a complete panic. Everybody was. Except for me, of course. So I went to the front of the ship with my spear, waited until it was up, up, up right at the top of the next wave and – sure enough – there it was. A sea monster. A real ugly-looking brute, about a mile long with a mouth as big as a snake pit. And it was thrashing about, see, trying to sink us so it could gobble us up. Anyway, I didn't waste a second. It was up to me to save everybody. So I took aim and I hurled my spear harder than I'd ever hurled it before. And it got him – chock! – right through the head. He rolled over once and sank down under the waves, all five miles of him, and the sea was calm again, and all my mates and the crew patting me on the back, and our Centurian saying I ought to be promoted... And yeah, well, anyway.

So we landed and marched and we finally ended up at the wall, ready for a bit of action, like. But what did we end up doing? Drilling, standing guard, hefting rocks about to patch up the pigging wall, but at least that kept us warm. And then things got warmer. Oh yes. Suddenly it was all happening. Late at night, it was. Suddenly this howling, ten times louder than the wind. And there they was, rushing us, hundreds of them, coming out of nowhere. Thousands. Clambering up the wall with their hair tied up and their paint on. Me and my mates come running from our post by the gates. You should've seen those barbarians fall back when they set eyes on me. They was chucking lighted torches over into the camp, see, and there was me with flames at my back. You should've heard them howl. I was fighting and jabbing and dodging and hacking but they still kept coming. Yeah. They just kept coming. Too many of them. Too many even for me. And with the other lads gone, well, that was it really. That's my story.

"How come," said Tom, "if you were such a brilliant fighter, you ended up dead?"

"Tom!" said Bella, shocked. But the ghost didn't seem to mind.

"I've often wondered that myself," he said. "And it was such a little wound, too." He began to unfasten his tunic. "Do you want to see?"

"No!" said Tom and Bella quickly and at the same time.

"It's kind of you to offer, though," added Bella. Even though she could already see he was a liar and a show-off, she couldn't help feeling quite sorry for him.

The soldier shook his head and sighed. "Just too many of them," he said, and then fell silent, sunk in thought.

Surprisingly, it was no trouble persuading him that he should stay in the children's bedroom out of the way for the rest of the day. Telling his story seemed to have calmed him down so that he was far easier to manage.

As the children were making their way down for breakfast they stopped for a moment on the stairs, looked at each other and grinned. "Honestly!" said Bella, trying to look outraged, but starting to laugh instead. "What a liar! All that stuff about the Emperor!"

"And a sea serpent!" sniggered Tom. "In the English Channel! And it grew four miles longer while he was telling us about it! What a nerve, expecting us to believe all that. How are we going to put up with him all the way to Rome?"

"Ignore him, I suppose," said Bella. "Like I do with you. But isn't he awful? And smelly! Now I know what that funny smell was in the car yesterday."

They looked at each other and both burst out laughing.

"It's cool, though, isn't it?" said Tom. "It's a really cool secret."

"I just hope he behaves himself," said Bella. "I'm not sure we know quite what we've let ourselves in for."

chapter four

*In which they cross the sea and
Tom gets a spot of good luck.*

The next two days passed surprisingly quickly. The ghost seemed quite content to spend most of his time in the children's bedroom, flicking through the picture books and setting up their toy soldiers in battle formations. When he did appear downstairs it was usually to follow Mum about with an admiring gleam in his eye. Once they caught him in the kitchen staring into a bowl of raw chicken livers that Mum had put out for the cat. When Tom demanded to know what he was up to, the soldier prodded a piece of the liver with his finger. "Just trying to see what sort of luck we're going to have on the journey," he muttered. "Could never get the hang of reading livers, though."

Tom glanced at Bella and she shrugged. "Come on, soldier," she said firmly. "Back upstairs."

They set off on Saturday, very early in the morning. Mum and Dad stood at the front door in their pyjamas to wave goodbye. The sun was hardly up and the house lights were still on, and the feeling of excitement reminded Bella of Christmas morning.

There was no opportunity to open the caravan door, so for the first part of the journey Tom persuaded the ghost to ride curled up on his side on the deep back window shelf of the car. "It's a good job Grandad can see right through him," Tom whispered to Bella as they both snuggled up either side of Auntie Eileen. The early morning air was quite chilly.

"Soon have you warmed up," said Grandad cheerfully as he turned on the heater. "Is everybody happy?"

"YES!" shouted Tom and Bella and Auntie Eileen. Grandma smiled and Grandad chuckled, and the car and caravan set off through the deserted streets and out into the countryside, heading for Dover.

But the ghost was not happy. He didn't like travelling by car now any more than he had last time, and they had gone many miles before he dared to open his eyes. And when he did, he shut them again quickly.

"Hey-up, mate," he said in alarm. "Looks like we're being followed."

Tom frowned. "What do you mean?"

"Didn't say anything, duckbod," said Auntie Eileen.

"Followed," insisted the ghost. "There's a pigging great thing right behind us. Another couple of minutes and it'll have us. Tell the Captain he's got to run faster!"

Tom sighed. He turned around, knelt up on the back seat and peered over the ghost.

"What is it?" Bella asked nervously.

There, filling almost the whole view from the back window, hurtling along behind the car, bouncing on the bumps in the road was – the Gypsy Belle.

"What's the matter with you?" Tom said to the ghost crossly. "Of *course* it's following us. It's the caravan. We're pulling it behind us."

Bella sighed with relief.

"Idiot," grumbled Tom, clambering down and sitting properly in the seat again.

"I don't suppose he can help it," said Bella kindly. "He's so nervous about travelling in the car that he's scared at the slightest thing."

"Now just a minute," said the ghost indignantly, shuffling again on his uncomfortable perch. "I'm just keeping a lookout, that's all. Just keeping an eye on my rear."

Tom sniggered. "No good having an eye on your rear," he said. "When you sit down you won't be able to see anything."

"Tom!" snapped Grandma. "I thought we'd agreed: no teasing Bella."

"I wasn't talking to Bella," said Tom indignantly.

"Well, I hope you weren't being rude to Auntie Eileen."

"He's just having a joke, darling," said Auntie Eileen, who never liked to hear anyone getting into trouble.

"Probably talking to himself again," said Grandad.

"Yes" said Bella, quickly. "He was. He's always talking to himself."

"Strange boy," said Grandad.

"You're laughing at me now," the ghost muttered darkly. "But I know about these things. You'll see. You'll be glad of me one of these days."

And, as it turned out, he was right.

They halted in a layby for breakfast. The ghost slid out of the car and stood a little way apart, clearly relieved that they'd stopped. When they'd all stretched their legs, they got back into the car to eat, leaving the ghost standing by the litter bin, keeping a suspicious eye on the passing traffic.

Grandma poured them all coffee from a flask and passed around fresh bread rolls with marmalade on them. "Only two more hours," said Grandad through a mouthful of bread, "and we'll be in Dover."

"Don't talk with your mouth full please, Grandad." said Grandma sternly. He turned to her, his mouth open to protest. "And keep your mouth closed while you're eating," she added. He closed it.

"How will we get the caravan on to the ship?" asked Bella, carefully swallowing her mouthful before she spoke.

"We just tow her on, of course," said Grandad. "Up a big ramp and into the bowels of the ship."

"Ugh," said Tom.

"Lovely coffee, Grandma," said Grandad. "Is there any more?"

There wasn't; but Auntie Eileen quickly thrust hers at him. "Here you are, duckbod," she said. "Have mine. I've had plenty." She waved her full cup under his nose. Grandad chuckled, embarrassed, and Grandma said firmly, "Drink it yourself, Eileen. And shut up."

But Auntie Eileen wasn't put off so easily. "Well, have one of these sweeties, then," she pleaded. "Go on. They'll stop you feeling thirsty. They're lovely, look. They're lemon ones."

Tom and Bella offered to have one each so that she wouldn't be disappointed. As they sucked them, they stared through the car window at the soldier, who was standing aimlessly on the damp grass in his shabby uniform, flinching whenever a big lorry rumbled by. He caught them looking at him and quickly straightened his shoulders. It made Bella feel sad. "Look at him," she whispered. "I'm glad we're taking him back where he belongs."

Tom nodded. "There's bound to be loads more ghosts there for him to talk to. In Latin, prob'ly."

Before they set off again, Grandad sent Tom into the caravan to make sure the curtains were still tied back securely so that he'd be able to see the road behind them in the rear-view mirror. This meant Tom was able to smuggle the ghost inside. "You'll be more comfortable in here," he said. "But don't touch anything."

They arrived in Dover just before lunchtime and joined the queue of cars and caravans waiting to board the ferry. Grandad reached under the dashboard and brought out a denim sailor's cap. He put it on, pulling the peak down jauntily over his forehead.

"*Oh-o-oh!*" he sang. "*A life on the ocean waves*
Is better than going to sea.
A life on the ocean waves
De dee de dee de dee."

And he drummed his fingers on the steering wheel in time to the song.

Tom and Bella lowered their windows. A fresh sea breeze whistled through the car and flapped the maps about on the back shelf. They could hear seagulls shrieking – Bella thought they sounded sad and Tom thought they sounded angry – and the growling of engines as more and more cars joined the queue.

Grandma began reading aloud from her Book of the Road: "Dover is an historic town with many…"

"Can we get out for a second?" asked Tom quickly.

Grandad turned and winked at them both. "Stay near the car, then," he said. "We'll be moving up soon."

The children slipped quickly round to the caravan and opened the door. Out tumbled the ghost on to the tarmac. "I've had enough!" he said furiously, getting to his feet. "Do you think that's any way for a soldier of the legions to travel?" he demanded. "Crushed between camp chairs with my foot in a bucket that smells of… of…? I should be up front. I should…" He stopped. They heard the noise of the seagulls again and the grumble of traffic and, below it all, the distant rush and crash of the waves. The children, who had drawn back from him, a bit afraid at his outburst, saw his expression change and soften. "The sea," he whispered.

"Yeah," said Tom. "And what a good job you got rid of that old sea serpent," he added sarcastically. "We've got nothing to worry about now, have we?"

The soldier sniffed and looked around him. Suddenly his eyes widened in alarm and he began backing towards the caravan, pointing with a quivering finger at something behind where the children were standing. They spun round quickly to look and were relieved to see nothing to worry about: just a low wall, some traffic signs and, perched on one of them, a chirpy-looking blue, black and white bird with a long tail.

"What's the matter now?" demanded Tom impatiently.

"There," said the ghost, stabbing the air with a pale finger. "An omen! A terrible omen!" He covered his face with his hands. "That's me finished," he mumbled. "I'll never get home now."

"It's that bird," said Bella. "That's what he's pointing at."

"Frightened of a bird?" said Tom scornfully. "What is it, anyway? Why's it an omen? Oh, I know. Maybe it's an omen pigeon." And he sniggered.

"It's a magpie," snapped Bella. "Shut up and stop being stupid. You can see he's frightened."

"No I'm not," squeaked the ghost. "I'm just, I'm just a bit…worried. And so should you be. Look, there it goes." And with a flap of its wings the magpie rose into the air and flew away inland. The soldier stared after it, shaking his head. "That was a real bad sign, that was. One magpie. By Jove! You'll not get me on that ship, not now."

"If you don't get on the ship," said Tom, "you don't get home. It's up to you."

"Look, mate, you don't understand. One magpie. Know what that means? Disaster! Storms, maybe. Sea monsters. Anything."

"One for sorrow!" said Bella suddenly. Tom looked at her, baffled. "You know," she said. "One for sorrow, two for joy. One magpie. One for sorrow, see." She turned to the ghost and took hold of his cold hand. "There was another one, you know," she said gently. "Behind the wall. Didn't you see it?"

The ghost looked at her, frowning.

"There was," she said. "That's two for joy. So there's nothing to worry about, is there? Come on."

The ghost smiled slowly. "Two? Two magpies? Ah, well, that's different then, i'n't it?"

The line of cars had begun to move and Grandad was shouting to the children to get back in. So they pulled the ghost into the car with them and this time Bella sat between his knees.

"There's our ship!" she shouted. "Look! Look! I can see it!" And so she could. Beyond the low buildings and cranes its red funnel towered above them in the sunshine. It was big – far bigger than they had even imagined.

Tom leaned across to Bella and whispered in her ear. "Hey, I didn't see another magpie."

"Neither did I," Bella whispered back. "But there was probably one around somewhere." And with a rattle and a clank the car pulled the caravan up the ramp and into the dark insides of the ship.

They left it down there and were soon all up on the top deck, the sea wind whipping their hair into their faces. As the ship pulled out of the harbour, they could see the white cliffs bright in the sunshine.

The soldier was leaning with his back to the rail, staring up at the funnel. "What gets me," he said, "is where they put the sails."

"It doesn't have sails," said Bella.

"Ah, I see," he said. "A galley, huh?" He turned and leaned right over the rail, peering down towards the water line. "Funny," he said. "Can't see any oars."

"It's got an engine, stupid," said Tom. "It prob'ly works the same way as the car."

"What?!" yelped the ghost in alarm. "He don't stick his feet through the bottom of this, surely? We'll all sink!" He glanced down at Grandad's feet, which were planted firmly on the deck. This seemed to reassure him, but he still looked worried.

"Off to the restaurant now, I think," said Grandad. "Order a bit of lunch, have a glass of wine. Come on, Grandma, Eileen. Let's get a table. You kiddies join us when you're ready, hey?"

As Grandad strolled off singing with his captain's cap pulled down tight to stop it blowing away, the ghost saluted smartly. The ship's engines rumbled. They could feel the deck vibrating under their feet. A flock of seagulls followed in their wake, crying and swooping low, and the two children and the ghost watched the white cliffs growing smaller and smaller and the sea grow wider and wider. "Rome," said the ghost to himself happily, "here I come."

One of the seagulls wheeling overhead swooped very low. Something white splashed on to Tom's head. "Ugh! Oh no!" he shouted. He wiped angrily at his hair with his sleeve. Bella doubled up with laughter. But the ghost just beamed with happiness. "Now *that*," he said, "is *very* lucky. Very lucky indeed."

chapter five

A haunting chapter in which the ghost grows gloomier and Tom and Bella get a nasty fright.

The crossing was quite calm after all, and when the ship had docked at Ostend, a voice over the loud speaker told them all to go to their cars. Grandad led the way and as he marched down the steps he was singing softly:

"What shall we do with the drunken sailor?
What shall we do with the drunken sailor?
Dee dee dee dee diddly dee dee…"

Grandma looked at him closely as they approached the car, and announced that she had better drive. This stopped the ghost in mid-stride. "Oh no," he said. "That's no good. Look at her short little legs. You ain't getting me in that car unless the Captain's driving."

"Don't be daft. She's a very good driver. The best, actually," said Tom. But still the ghost hung back.

"You sure there was two magpies?" he demanded.

"Certain," said Bella. "Now get in."

They drove out of the cool dark hold and into the afternoon sunshine. Men in dark uniforms directed them into the right lane and, after a brief glance at their passports, waved them on into the town.

"You sure that ship didn't just go round in a circle?" asked the ghost suspiciously, peering out of the window from his perch on the back shelf. "This all looks just the same to me."

But, to the excited children, everything looked quite different. The houses were taller and narrower, and leaned together shoulder to shoulder. The shops had their awnings pulled down, bright and stripy in the sunshine with words written on them that they couldn't understand. And the cars that whizzed by on the other side of the road had strange cluttered number plates.

"I should drive on the right, if I were you, Grandma," advised Grandad.

"You just concentrate on holding the map the right way up," said Grandma sternly, "and leave the driving to me." Auntie Eileen, nursing the bottle of eggnog she'd bought on the ferry, smiled in her sleep and began to snore.

Ostend was full of holiday-makers. They strolled the streets in their summer clothes, some of them smiling and waving to see the Gypsy Belle roll by. The ghost waved back at them, graciously but invisibly, from the back window.

"Is he a big man here, then, the Captain?" he asked; and added as an afterthought, "Where are we anyway? Gaul?"

"Belgium," said Tom.

"Belgium." The ghost rolled the word around his tongue and then said loudly, "You don't mean these are the Belgae?" he stared out of the window at the smiling faces. "What's happened to them? I served with some of them on the Wall. A right crowd of villains. Belgae!" He whistled. "By Jove!"

They left Ostend behind and sped through the flat countryside and long, strung-out villages. The ghost fell silent and Grandad fell asleep, and the children sang through all the songs they could remember, including one about a flea on a feather on a bird on an egg in a nest on a twig on a branch on a tree, that went on for mile after mile.

It was dark when they got to their campsite near the German border. They pulled up at the office by the entrance gates and Grandad and Tom went inside to pay for their night's stay. They gave their name to the elderly woman behind the desk and showed her their booking form. She nodded and looked enquiringly out of the window at the car. Grandad cleared his throat. "Er…twaz adults and dur er…bambinos," he said, and beamed proudly at Tom.

"Three adults and two children?" repeated the woman in perfect English. "Thank you, sir. And enjoy your stay."

Grandad touched his sailor's cap politely and led Tom back to the car.

"Hey, Grandma," said Tom, "do you know what? Grandad spoke in French!"

"That's what you call it, is it?" said Grandma.

They unhitched the caravan under some trees, and while Grandma and Auntie Eileen went inside to sort out the beds, Grandad, Tom and Bella, by the light of an oil lamp, put up the awning. It was like a big tent that fastened to the side of the van and it was where Grandad was to sleep.

The ghost, who, Tom noticed for the first time, gave off a rather eerie glow in the darkness, hovered about uselessly, glancing now and again over his shoulder as though expecting company, and saluting every time Grandad passed him. When Tom went across to the tap with a bucket and a torch to fetch some water, the ghost went with him.

"How do you feel?" asked Tom pleasantly. "The first bit of the journey's over now. We'll be in Rome in a few days."

The ghost was slouching along with his head down and his big luminous feet scuffing the ground. He sighed heavily.

"What's the matter, now?" said Tom. "You should be happy."

"Happy?" said the ghost. "Huh!" And he gave a hollow laugh. "It's no good, mate. You done your best. But you don't understand."

"Don't understand what?" demanded Tom impatiently. He turned on the tap and stood back so as not to get splashed.

"It's seeing all you lot together," said the ghost. "You're all family, aren't you? But what about me? I don't fit in nowhere. All my mates are gone. And I don't understand things no more."

"But you've got me," said Tom. "I'm your mate."

The ghost shook his head. "You're just a kid," he said sadly.

Tom felt hurt. He said nothing but turned off the tap angrily and began hauling the heavy bucket back to the caravan. The ghost trailed after him, still looking miserable. "Listen," he said. "I'm sorry. You *are* a good mate. It's just not the same, that's all." But Tom had decided he was never going to speak to him again.

When they got back to the caravan the awning was up and looking cosy and Grandma had made some hot chocolate. Inside the caravan it was warm and snug, the gas lamps hissing softly. The children sat on their sleeping bags and drank their hot chocolate while Grandma read to them from a booklet all about the site, translating as she went:

"This site is set in what were once the grounds of a great house. The ruins of the house are still to be seen to the west of the site. These ruins are said to be haunted…" Here, Tom and Bella snapped out of their separate daydreams and began to pay attention. "…by a beautiful lady in white," Grandma continued. "The story goes that she was abandoned by her lover on their wedding day, and so pined away and died of a broken heart. She is said to have been seen, even by recent visitors, wandering the ruins at night in her white wedding dress."

"Better lock the door tonight then, eh?" said Grandad. "Don't want her wandering in here. We're a bit overcrowded as it is."

"Shall I read on?" asked Grandma, looking at him sternly over her glasses.

"No thanks," they all said at once.

But the children were not the only ones whose ears had pricked up at the mention of the White Lady. The Roman, squashed between the bunkbeds and the cooker, was rubbing his bristly chin and looking very thoughtful. Suddenly, with a wink and a grin at the children, he went to the door, opened it and slipped out into the night.

The grownups all turned quickly and stared at the door. Auntie Eileen shivered. "Oh dear," she said, and reached for her eggnog.

"Who came in last?" demanded Grandma. "Whoever it was obviously didn't shut the door properly."

Grandad got up quickly, shut the door and locked

it. "Must've been the wind," he said casually. "Nothing to worry about."

"He'll have to stay out there now," whispered Tom to Bella.

A little later, walking across to the shower block with their toothbrushes, they made plans. "I vote we go and see if we can find her," said Tom. "We're good at seeing ghosts, and she'd make a good friend for him. Stop him going on about being lonely all the time."

Bella wasn't so sure. "She might not be very nice," she said.

"Well, what could she do to us?" said Tom scornfully. "I mean, if a great big Roman soldier can't hurt us, how could she? She's just some woman in a white dress who's a bit depressed."

"We'd have to wait until they're all asleep, though," said Bella. "And then sneak out past Grandad."

So that's what they decided to do.

Tom and Bella slept in bunks at one end of the caravan, Grandma and Auntie Eileen shared the big pull-down bed at the other end, and Grandad slept on an old blow-up bed in the awning. It always took him a long time to inflate his bed, and they could still hear him pumping it up with the foot pump and singing along in time, long after they'd snuggled down.

*"**Blow** the wind **southerly, southerly, southerly**
Blow the wind **southerly...**"*

At long last all was quiet, save for the even breathing from the other end of the Gypsy Belle and the exhausted snoring from Grandad in the awning.

Now, the children knew that Grandma always slept with one eye open. And anyone who's tried sleeping in a caravan knows that it's not easy to get out of bed without putting your foot in something you shouldn't, or setting the whole van rocking like a fair ride. But carefully, carefully, the two of them managed to creep to the door and, pulling the catch back silently, they slipped out and through the awning, helping themselves to the two torches that hung by the awning door.

The night air was sharp and cold, but they had their track suits on, so only their faces felt the chill. The moon was up and the stars were bright, and over to the west they could see the broken ruins of the great house black and jagged against the sky.

They made their way between the dark and silent tents and caravans until they came to the low crumbling wall that marked the boundary between the campsite and the ruins. The pools of light thrown by their torches made everywhere around them look darker and blacker still. Shadows seemed to lean and jump as they walked slowly between the towering walls and tumbled heaps of stones. Tall weeds and low branches touched them with limp night-time leaves as they passed. The caravan seemed very far away.

Suddenly, Bella stopped and caught hold of Tom's arm. "I don't want to go any further," she said. Tom didn't argue. They were close to the tallest of the ruined walls now, the walls they'd seen from a distance. Closer up, they looked less jagged but huge, towering against the night sky, blocking the stars. Tom shone his torch ahead and they could see each stone in the old wall with mosses and tiny plants growing in their crumbling corners.

"Birds!" whispered Bella in surprise. "Look!"

But they weren't birds swooping around the walls with ragged wings. They were bats. And there seemed to be hundreds of them, flitting through the dark.

Bella tugged at Tom's arm again. "Come on. Let's go. I don't like this. It's creepy."

They turned and began heading back the other way. But before they'd gone far it began to dawn on them horribly that they didn't recognise anything. The ruins blocked their view in every direction and they had no idea which way the campsite lay.

Tom stood still, breathing noisily. Bella tried to drag him forward. "Come on! Which way?"

"I don't know," hissed Tom. "Shut up a minute."

They stood there in the dark, shining their torches around them crazily. "This way, I think," said Tom, and they began to run, crashing against the bushes and dodging the tall stones. But it was no good. Everywhere looked the same. Bella began to cry and Tom found himself shouting in a wobbly voice: "Grandad?! Grandad!"

Suddenly there was a scraping sound and a rattling of stones somewhere just behind them. They whirled round but saw nothing. Bella dodged behind the nearest pile of masonry, dragging Tom with her. They crouched there in the dark, listening. Was it the spooky White Lady? Was it their own grumpy ghost? Was it maybe Grandad come to rescue them?

Then, from the same direction as the first sound, they heard a steady crunching noise, which grew louder. Tom thought it might be someone walking over stones but Bella had a different idea. "She's eating s—somebody!" she whispered, horrified. "She's ch— chewing them up! Listen!"

From out of the dark ruins the sound came again. Crunch. Crunch. Crunch. Tom felt the hair on the back of his neck begin to bristle. His hands, gripping the torch, felt wet and sweaty. "Shut up!" he hissed at Bella furiously. "It's prob'ly only…"

But he got no further. For at that moment a dreadful blood-curdling wail broke the night: "Aaaaaaaiiiiiiiiiiiiiighh!" and echoed between the crumbling walls. The children clung to one another as the sound soaked slowly into the old stones and died away.

Then, suddenly, crashing clumsily out of the murky shadows, came – something. Something big that stared about it wildly in the torchlight and snorted as it breathed. Bella could control herself no longer. She took a deep breath and bellowed into the night as loudly as she could: "HELP!"

chapter six

*In which one mystery is solved and
the children are faced with another.*

The thing, whatever it was, turned its head sharply in their direction. It was too late to run. Tom shone his torch at it, hoping he might dazzle it. And he did. But there was no need. For there, in the torchlight, was a face probably more terrified than his own. And he recognised it. It belonged to one of the other campers, a big, round-faced man, who he'd seen earlier chatting to Grandad outside the shower block.

"Quick!" the man gasped now. "Give me your torch! Let's get out of here! I've seen her and she's horrible! Horrible!" And, hoisting the children to their feet, he led the way at a shambling pace out of the ruins. "What are you doing here, anyway?" he wheezed as they jogged along. "You shouldn't be out on your own at this time of night."

"We came looking for the White Lady," panted Tom, trying to keep up.

"So did I," moaned the man.

"Do you believe in ghosts, then?" puffed Bella. It was her experience that grownups always said they didn't, even if they really did.

"Oh yes," said the man breathlessly. "I'd never seen one before, and now I hope I never will again. I'm making a study of the haunted sites of Western Europe. But that's it now, though. I'm going home. I couldn't stand to see anything like that White Lady again. She was horrible."

"Was she eating somebody?" Bella asked hopefully. She was interested to know, now that they were almost safe again.

The man wiped a hand over his face and shuddered. "Not when I saw her," he said. "I only caught a glimpse, mind. But that was enough for me. She was all green and glowing in the dark. The guidebook said she was supposed to have pined away, but she was enormous! She had great bulging muscles. And ugly? I've never seen such a big nose and so many bristles on a woman. And I don't know *what* had happened to her wedding dress. It didn't even cover her knees, and she had these great hairy legs." He shuddered again. "No wonder her boyfriend ran off on their wedding day. I don't blame him."

The children grew thoughtful. That description

seemed familiar. It seemed to fit someone they knew quite well.

"Anyway, you get back to your caravan now. Your family will be worried about you. And don't you go near those ruins again, do you hear?"

"Thank you for rescuing us," said Bella. They all three wished one another good night and the man walked away to his own caravan, still muttering to himself: "Horrible. Horrible."

Luckily, no-one had missed them. The next morning, Tom found the ghost lounging against the side of the car, looking a little pale in the sunshine.

"Did you find her, then?" Tom asked slyly.

"Nah." The ghost shook his head in disgust. "I *thought* I'd found her. I could hear something scrabbling about. But then I come face to face with this fat-faced bloke who takes one look at me, screams, and goes running off. Ha! And if you ask me," he went on, although Tom hadn't, "there i'n't no lady. I'd have found her if there was. Nah, there's nobody for me, mate. Nobody in the whole wide world."

They travelled south all that day until the children, although still excited to be on holiday, became very restless from sitting so long in the car. The weather was getting warmer and warmer and they had all the car windows open to keep cool. Grandad had changed into his khaki shorts and the sun, beating through the windscreen, was turning his knees pink. Grandma had wrapped some tea towels round her shoulders so that the draught from the windows wouldn't give her a stiff neck, and Auntie Eileen had tied a plastic rain hat on her head to stop her hair blowing about.

Tom and Bella were playing at waving at people and counting how many waved back. After the twenty-fourth and twenty-fifth returned wave (from a pair of hikers in leather shorts), Tom began asking whether they were going to stop soon. He couldn't help feeling a bit anxious about the ghost, who had been packed in the caravan since early that morning.

"Listen, Tommy Tucker," said Grandad over his shoulder. "If we press on today, we can camp by the Rhine tonight. Have a swim. Run about. How's that, eh?"

"What's the Rhine?" asked Tom.

"Sewer of Europe," said Grandma.

"Oh dear," said Auntie Eileen, adding quickly, "but I expect it's a very nice sewer."

"It was called a sewer," said Grandma sternly, "because everybody poured their rubbish into it."

"Not any more, they don't," said Grandad.

"And I expect it's very nice all the same," repeated Auntie Eileen soothingly. She passed a bag of humbugs round, popped one in her own mouth, and settled back with a smile.

Eventually, around teatime, they reached their next campsite. Tom was, by now, very concerned about the ghost, and while Grandad was taking their passports to the site office he hurried round to the caravan as fast as his cramped legs would go. When he opened the door the ghost almost fell on top of him. He looked hot and confused and not in the best of moods.

"What's going on?" he demanded gruffly. "Where are we? What's happening?"

"It's alright," said Tom. "We're staying here tonight. I couldn't let you out before. We only stopped for toilets."

But the long day travelling seemed to have muddled the ghost alarmingly. He staggered about, staring around him. "What's going on?" he said again. "I don't like it here."

"That river over there," said Tom, pointing, "Is called the Rhinoceros or the Rhino or something. Big German river, anyway."

"German?" The ghost seemed to churn this piece of information over. Slowly, his eyes widened with horror. "Germania? Not Germania!" he yelped, and dived back into the Gypsy Belle. And at that moment Grandad, back at the car, called over to Tom, "Stop waving your arms about! Look sharp and shut that door. It's starting to rain!"

So Tom slammed the door and sprinted back to the car through the slow but heavy drops of summer rain that fell faster and faster until, by the time he and Grandad were safely back inside the car, it had become a downpour that drummed on the car roof with a noise like marbles.

"Mustn't go jumping out of the car like that," said Grandad sternly. "Mustn't go opening caravan doors. Ask first, eh?" He sighed and turned to Grandma. "World of his own," he said. "Talking to the caravan door. Just talking away to it!"

"Sometimes," said Grandma, "I think I would get more sense if *I* talked to a door."

Grandad looked hurt.

"People think I'm talking to myself sometimes," said Auntie Eileen. "But I'm actually talking to Ron."

"Ron's dead, Eileen," snapped Grandma.

Tom and Bella had never met Uncle Ron, but they knew he'd been Auntie Eileen's husband.

"What do you say to him?" asked Bella, who was always interested in this sort of thing.

"Well," said Auntie Eileen, "I say things like, *You would never take me on holiday, Ron. But now you're dead and I'm off to Rome. So hard luck.* Just little things like that."

"And what does he say?" asked Bella.

"That'll do Bella," said Grandma.

"Well, nothing duckbods," said Auntie Eileen. "That's the beauty of it. He can't say anything now, can he?"

Grandad clapped his hands together noisily. "Right," he said. "Come on! Let's get the van into position."

They towed the Gypsy Belle to a quiet grassy spot between the wide fast-flowing river and the dark dripping pine trees. Grandad, with a plastic raincoat over his shoulders, unhitched her and wound down her feet. Then the rest of them made a dash for it across the squishy grass.

Grandma got there first. As she flung back the door, Tom saw the Roman ghost start up in terror from the floor, roll over and make a grab for his sword.

"It's us!" shouted Tom. "It's us! It's only us!"

The ghost's hand dropped to his side and he wiped the other across his face. Grandma turned in the doorway and gave Tom a long look. He grinned at her foolishly and shrugged.

"Potty," pronounced Grandma. "Quite potty."

Grandad came puffing up behind them. "Go on," he urged. "Get in. We're all getting wet. And you don't need the potty. There's a toilet block just over there. And showers. The lot. Very nice."

They all squeezed in and watched Grandad getting wet as he made several journeys moving stuff from the caravan to the car to make more room. He had decided not to put up the awning because it would only have to be packed up wet the next morning.

Gloomily, Bella watched the sheets of rain melting into the wide river. "What if it floods?" she said suddenly. "We'll float away. We'll be like Noah's Ark."

Tom laughed. The ghost, keeping out of the way on top of the fold-down cooker, moaned and buried his face in his hands.

"Do you know?" said Auntie Eileen brightly. "I didn't think it rained abroad. I thought it was always sunny. Aren't I silly?"

"Yes," said Grandma.

At last Grandad joined them. They all squeezed together on the long seats either side of the table and stared out at the rain. They were tired with travelling, and the holiday excitement wasn't brand new anymore.

The grey river churned by. The pine trees dripped. The sky was the colour of mucky sheets. Bella didn't like the place at all, but didn't want to say so. Tom was less polite, "P'raps we shouldn't stop here," he suggested casually. "P'raps we should…" he groped for an expression he'd heard Grandad use: "…press on. P'raps we should drive all night."

"Nonsense!" said Grandad cheerily. "Splendid place. Plenty of shade. Plenty of space."

"Plenty of rain," said Grandma.

"It's a very good site," insisted Grandad. "Very interesting, too. Very historical. Let me get the brochure."

Tom and Bella glanced at one another and sighed. Both of them felt there was something miserable about the place and that they wouldn't have been particularly happy here even if the sun was shining.

And the ghost didn't help matters. There he sat now, knees drawn up to his big bristly chin, flinching and staring about him every time a particularly heavy drip fell with a plunk on the caravan roof.

Bella got out a pack of cards and the children began to play. The ghost was forced to move when Grandma got up to boil a kettle. He settled himself grumpily beside Tom, who gave him a nudge and told him to cheer up.

"Leave him," said Bella softly. "He's sulking."

"Oh, don't sulk, duckybods," said Auntie Eileen to Grandad. "Here, have a sweetie."

"Sulk?" said Grandad indignantly. "I'm not sulking. Why would I sulk? This site is splendid." And he went into a sulk.

After a few minutes he stood up and took a deep breath. "Going out for a walk," he announced. "Rain's easing off a bit. Going to explore."

"And me," said Tom quickly. He struggled back into his cagoul. Everyone had to budge and shuffle round to let Tom and Grandad out.

"You go with them," Bella urged the ghost in a whisper. She couldn't bear to be cooped up with his misery any longer. "They might need you," she added cunningly.

The ghost wiped his nose with the back of his hand and stood up slowly as though his joints needed oiling. Then he walked straight through the table and out of the side of the Gypsy Belle to join Grandad and

Tom on the grass outside. Bella was shocked. He'd never done anything like that before. Whatever could be wrong with him?

Tom and Grandad walked in silence for some way along the bank of the river until they came to a wooden fence that ran down to the water's edge and marked the boundary of the campsite. Then they turned and strolled back in the other direction, passing the caravan again. Tom could see Bella's pale face pressed against the steamed-up window, and he gave her a wave. The river roared past with a noise like a distant motorway, and Grandad began singing in his growly voice:

> *"Row, row, row your boat*
> *Gently down the stream.*
> *Merrily, merrily, merrily..."*

"It's great, isn't it?" said Tom.

"Superb," agreed Grandad. "Can't let a drop of rain spoil the day. Water off a duck's back, eh?"

"Grandad, why does Auntie Eileen call everybody duckbods?"

"Just her way," said Grandad.

Tom looked behind and saw the ghost following them at a distance, glancing from side to side, one hand ready on his sword, and muttered to himself: "Idiot."

"I beg your pardon?" said Grandad, looking at him sharply.

"I mean they're all idiots," lied Tom quickly, "for not liking the rain and that."

Grandad shook his head. "Don't know what they're missing," he said sadly. "And look at this." He pulled the site brochure from his cagoul pocket. "Very interesting history, this place."

Tom was surprised to see that there was a little drawing of a Roman soldier in the bottom right hand corner of the brochure, dressed in a uniform very much like the ghost's. However, the soldier in the picture looked far smarter, with a nicely pressed cloak and spotless armour. He had rather a silly-looking face, a bit like a doll, and Tom decided that on the whole he preferred his own Roman, who at that moment was shuffling miserably through the grass behind them.

"*…on their march north,*" Grandad was reading, "*the legion found themselves under constant attack from fierce and fearless Germanic tribes. In this very spot they made their camp, unaware that they had chosen a grove sacred to the Germanic tree gods. That night the tribes attacked. Taken by surprise and heavily outnumbered, much of the legion was destroyed. A few survivors fled north, escaping the slaughter but never able to live down the shame of having left their comrades to die.* Crikey! Stirring stuff, eh? They've excavated just up here. Found arrow heads, skulls, that sort of thing."

"Wow!" said Tom, who had actually been listening this time. "Can we have a look? Can we try and dig something up?"

"Steady on," laughed Grandad. "And listen to this. Your Grandma'll like this: *Walkers in the woods at night have reported screams and sounds of battle; and many people have claimed to see the ghostly legion silently marching between the trees.* What a load of old rubbish. That makes two sites in a row advertising ghosts. They must think we're daft."

But Tom had stopped listening. He had an idea, and the more he thought about it, the less he liked it. He looked again at the ghost, who stood with shoulders hunched miserably against the rain. As they passed him to walk back to the caravan it seemed he could hardly pull himself to attention. Something was making him very miserable indeed. And Tom now had an awful feeling that he knew what it might be.

chapter seven

*A short chapter in which
the ghost meets some old mates.*

Tom and Bella and Auntie Eileen stood in the washroom cleaning their teeth. The children liked to do this with Auntie Eileen because they were fascinated by the way she cleaned hers. She actually took them out of her mouth and held them, smiling whitely in one hand, the gums all shiny and pink, while she scrubbed a toothbrush around them with the other.

She saw them watching her. "You need to clean your teeth well and look after them," she said. "And then you won't have to have silly teeth like these." Her face looked quite different when her teeth were out, and her voice didn't sound the same. But she soon popped them back in and flashed them at the children. "That's it," she said. "Now I'm going to help Grandma make us some lovely cocoa. So don't be too long."

"Go on, then," said Bella to Tom as soon as the door had swung closed. "Why do you think he's so miserable at the moment? Do you think he knows a lot of Roman soldiers were killed near here? Or do you think he just sort of feels it? Cos I do. I think this whole place feels dark and sad."

"I dunno," said Tom, screwing the cap back on the toothpaste. "But I've got a feeling it's more than that."

"Well, I miss him boasting," said Bella. "I miss him being big-headed. I'd rather have him fibbing and showing off than looking sad all the time."

"I bet he goes off to that wood tonight," said Tom. "And if he does, I'm going to follow him."

"Oh, Tom. Don't. *I'm* not going to. Look what happened last time we sneaked out."

"Who cares?" said Tom. "I'll go on my own, then."

When they got back to the caravan they found a big discussion going on about where everybody should sleep. Without the awning for Grandad, space for sleeping was rather cramped.

"What about this?" Grandad was saying. "Bella and Tom and Eileen in the big bed, Grandma and me in the bunks?"

"No, no, no," said Grandma. "That's no good. We'll have Eileen, Bella and myself in the big bed and you and Tom in the bunks."

"I could sleep on the floor," offered Auntie Eileen. "I wouldn't mind."

"Shut up, Eileen," said Grandma.

"What about," said Grandad, "Eileen and Bella having the bunks, because they're small; and you and me and Tom having the bed?"

"Absolutely not," said Grandma briskly. "I've told you what we're doing. Now get the beds made up."

Grandad eyed the bottom bunk uncomfortably, sighed, and went to fetch the sleeping bags. Tom smiled with relief. Stuck between Grandma and Grandad in the big bed, he would have had no chance at all of sneaking out into the night.

Grandad turned out the gas lights, shuffled himself backwards into the bottom bunk and almost immediately began to snore. Tom gave the others plenty of time to get to sleep before he crept out. Even Bella had got tired of listening for him and was breathing deeply and evenly, snuggled between Grandma and Auntie Eileen in the big bed.

Outside, the rain had stopped, although heavy drops were still plopping from the branches to the ground here and there. The river seemed to make less noise in the darkness, as though it was afraid of waking something up. And as Tom walked away from the caravan, he thought how new and small and alone it looked, crouched between the old river and the ancient forest.

He hadn't seen the ghost since the afternoon walk with Grandad, but Tom had a good idea where he would find him. He made his way cautiously between the first few trees and, sure enough, there was the soldier, leaning against a broad tree trunk and giving off an eerie glow that cast no shadow. Tom flashed his torch at him, and the ghost swung round in alarm. When he saw it was Tom he seemed to relax. But still he didn't smile. "What are you doing here?" he hissed. "You get back quick, or you'll have the Captain after you."

"I'm not going back till you do," said Tom. "I'm not going back till you tell me what's wrong."

The ghost was looking around anxiously. He seemed impatient, on edge, as though he was expecting someone. "Look," he said, "just go back, will yer? If you're me mate you'll do that for me."

"Why?" asked Tom, watching him closely. "What are you waiting for? I bet I know."

The ghost turned on him furiously. "Will you just go back and…" He broke off suddenly and stood quite still. "Too late," he whispered miserably. "It's too late. They're here. Get down!" He shoved Tom to the ground and dived down beside him on the damp ground.

At first Tom saw nothing. And then, far away between the trees, a faint glow began to flicker, greenish-white. As it grew nearer it took on shape, blurred at first, but gradually becoming clearer. It was a long column of men – a huge army it seemed to Tom – marching together in step. And he saw that they didn't really flicker at all, but that as they passed behind and between the dark trees and the vanished trees that had grown there long ago, their light was interrupted, so that they seemed to move strangely, like figures in an old film.

They were Roman, no doubt about that. They stared straight ahead of them as they marched and their tramping feet made no sound on the forest floor. There was no creak of leather or clinking of weapons. They marched past, grim and silent, rank after rank of them. Tom could hear his own heart hammering in his chest. This was far too strange. He didn't like it, and yet it was somehow exciting. He wanted to be in there with them, beating a drum, maybe, marching along.

He felt the ghost rise to a crouch beside him coiled for action, and then suddenly with no warning springing to his feet and stumbling towards the marching army. "Wait for me, lads!" he cried. "I've come back! I never meant to leave you! Wait for me!"

But the marching men marched on, their gaze fixed straight ahead.

"I'm sorry!" howled the ghost, throwing out his arms. "But I've come back now! I'm still yer mate!"

There was no sign that the soldiers could even hear him. The ghost was trying to clutch at them now as they marched by him: an arm here, a sleeve there; but his grasp passed right through them.

At last someone did seem to notice him. A tall man broke from the ranks and walked towards the ghost, appearing more solid for a moment. He looked a little bit like Grandad, but sterner-looking and

with much darker skin. The ghost immediately drew himself to attention. "Permission to join you, sir?" he croaked, his voice hoarse from all his shouting.

The officer stared coldly at him for a moment and then, in a boomy, echoey voice that sounded as though it was trapped in a well, he said something in a language that Tom couldn't understand. The ghost appeared to repeat his request, falteringly, in the same language

Don't let him, thought Tom, crossing his fingers. *Don't let him join them.* He couldn't bear to think of his mate, the ghost, becoming one of those silent blank-faced men, marching for ever and ever through the dark grim trees.

chapter eight

In which the family runs into danger – and not the sort of danger that Grandma was worrying about.

With a curt shake of his head the officer turned on his heel and re-joined the ranks of soldiers, falling into step and disappearing gradually into the distance. They had almost passed by now. The ghost still stood stiffly, his back to Tom, until the last men were just a flicker again between the trees, their light already fading. Then the ghost's arm dropped limply to his side and Tom realised he had been holding it across his chest in a Roman salute until they'd gone. "Cheers, mates," he heard him whisper. And when he turned, Tom saw two luminous green tears trickling down his unshaven cheeks.

He saw Tom looking and brushed them away hurriedly with the back of his hand. "They wouldn't have me back," he said gruffly, and sniffed.

Tom shrugged. "Well," he said, "they looked a pretty miserable lot to me. What would you want to go back to them for? You're coming with us to Rome, remember? Rome!"

The ghost sniffed again and turned away. "Yeah," he said. "I'm going to Rome. But they ain't going to Rome, are they? They're never going to Rome. It's like I'm running away all over again."

"You?" teased Tom. "Running away? You, who fights sea monsters and all that?"

"Don't," growled the ghost.

"But if they were so good and brave, how come they're all ghosts now, marching through this wood for ever?"

"I never said they was good," muttered the ghost. He had stopped crying. "We weren't good. We was a right load of villains, all of us."

"Well, then."

"That's not the point!" the ghost shouted. "They wouldn't have me back! They think I'm a coward. But I'll show 'em. I will!"

"Course you will," said Tom.

"Yeah," said the ghost. "I'll show 'em. And I'll show you. I won't be letting no mates down no more, I won't. You'll see."

The next morning, they set off early as usual and called at a service station to fill up with petrol before heading south again. Tom went in with

Grandad to pay. While they were queuing, he took the opportunity to ask Grandad if they could play Monopoly again soon. Grandad had been the winner by miles last night, and Tom wanted another chance to beat him. He really didn't like not winning. Sometimes when he didn't win at a boardgame he would lose his temper and tip the board over, scattering all the pieces. This meant that Mum often let him win, just to avoid a fuss. But Grandad never did. Because Grandad liked winning too.

"You were piling up so much money last night," Tom said. "Thousands and thousands. There was hardly any room on the table for all your banknotes."

"I know," said Grandad smugly. "The secret is to make sure you own lots of hotels. Having all the hotels, that's how I end up having more money than the bank."

Just picturing all those little red house-shaped hotels set out all over the Monopoly board made Tom feel grumpy. And, what's more, it was bad enough having the ghost showing off and boasting all over the place without Grandad doing it, too. It was embarrassing because people were clearly listening; especially the four men in suits who were standing behind them in the queue. Tom hoped they didn't understand English and wouldn't realise Grandad was being big-headed. But just to be on the safe side he quickly changed the subject by asking for a chocolate bar as Grandad moved forward to pay.

Finally, they left the gloom behind them and travelled on into the sunshine. By the time they stopped again that night they were in Switzerland with everyone smiling and the weather so sunny that they were able to eat tea outside under the awning.

In Tom's opinion, one of the most interesting things about leaving the UK was the change of money. Every time Grandad marched into the site office with a little bundle of UK bank notes and came out again carrying money that looked quite different, it was another reminder that they really were on an adventure and a long way from home.

"It's a lot more interesting than our money," said Tom, examining the notes that Grandad had changed for him from the pocket money he'd saved. He tucked them away in his smart plastic wallet. Auntie Eileen, however, didn't agree.

"I don't like them," she said.

"Why not?" asked Bella, putting her own away in the little blue purse she'd knitted herself.

"They haven't got the Queen's head on, have they, duckbod?" said Auntie Eileen. "Don't you think that must hurt her feelings?"

This campsite they were on now was not much more than a field, which they were sharing with several other caravans and a lot of big brightly-coloured tents. After tea they got the Monopoly out again and started another long game. As it grew dark, moths began to fly in and beat their wings against the oil lamp that hung in the awning, as though they were trying to put it out. Through the open flap they could see the moon rise over the open fields.

The ghost seemed to have left his moodiness behind him on the Rhine. He hung around Tom and Bella eagerly like a waiter in a posh restaurant, laughing whenever anyone cracked a joke and saluting smartly every time Grandad glanced, unseeing, in his direction. He even so far forgot himself as to politely pull out a chair for Grandma when she returned from the toilets. She stared at the canvas seat – apparently moving on its own – and then looked at Grandad sharply. "Is this thing safe?" she demanded.

"Sorry! I moved it back for you with my foot," lied Tom quickly.

"Sit down!" hissed Bella at the ghost. "Stop hovering!"

He did as he was told.

When it was almost bedtime, Grandma went into the caravan to make the cocoa and to boil up some water. Grandad swirled his brandy around in his glass and held it up to the moon. "A very thorough woman, your Grandma," he said carefully. "Always boils the water, y'know. Every drop, south of Dover. Even for washing her feet. You have to admire a woman like that."

"And you should be grateful I do," shouted Grandma from inside the caravan. "Or do you want to catch something nasty?" And she began to recite her favourite list of dreaded diseases: "Typhoid, dysentery, worms…"

"Measles?" suggested Bella. Grandad snorted into his glass.

"But Grandma," said Tom, "everybody else here seems alright and I bet they all drink the water without boiling it."

"Used to it," snapped Grandma. "Besides, how do you *know* they're alright? Have you asked them?"

They all had to admit that they had not, and so they meekly drank their bedtime cocoa and Grandad went into the caravan to help Grandma set out the beds.

Tom stretched his legs and sighed. "I suppose we'd better tidy away," he said. The Monopoly board was a mess, with pretend money and little houses everywhere. No-one had won this time. Everyone had got fed up before the game finished.

The ghost pounced forward eagerly. "I'll do it, mate," he offered.

But they'd all forgotten that Auntie Eileen was still there. She watched in astonishment, gripping her glass of eggnog, as the Monopoly cards appeared to shuffle themselves into a pile and jump into the box. The dice and markers rattled in after them. The houses and hotels leapt into the air, hovered all together and then poured into the box like cereals into a bowl. The bank notes gathered themselves together from all over the table and dealt themselves out into piles according to their colour. The piles wriggled into elastic bands and flew into the box. Finally, the lid swooped up from under the table, floated for a moment and then dropped neatly into place.

The ghost dusted his hands together and beamed luminously at Tom and Bella. "There!" he said proudly. "I did that good, di'n't I?" But the children were holding their breath and watching Auntie Eileen as she stared at the tidy table in front of her.

She blinked a few times and then put down her empty glass. "I say, duckbods," she called shakily to Grandma, "do you think there's something wrong with this eggnog? Do you think I ought to boil it before I drink it?"

The next morning there was a great feeling of excitement as they set off. Today they were going to cross the Alps, the mountains which lay between them and Italy. They would go so high, Grandad told them, that they would see snow either side of the road even though it was summer. And the car would have to work very hard to pull the caravan all the way up and over – particularly, he hinted, as Grandma had packed so many tins of mince. "But you'll get us there, old thing, won't you?" he said, giving the car bonnet a friendly pat.

They drove for several hours through the morning sunshine and were already high in the mountains when they stopped for their elevenses. The ghost had taken it upon himself to be their rear-guard again, and was travelling on the rear window ledge, keeping a wary lookout. Now they'd stopped, he was pacing the perimeter of the layby and peering down over the edge at the road. It snaked away down, down, down, doubling back and forth on itself, growing narrower as it wound down the way they had come, till it looked like a ribbon and then a thin string unwinding far, far below. The sun glinted on tiny cars climbing the mountain behind them.

"Isn't he funny?" whispered Bella to Tom. "He's acting all important."

Indeed, the ghost did look rather silly, marching fiercely about, behaving as though he was defending a fort rather than a holiday picnic place with no-one else about.

Tom threw a pebble at a tree, and missed. "I thought he was going to be really good fun," he complained. "I thought: *Great! Take a ghost on holiday. Just think of the amazing tricks we could play!* But he's been miserable and he's been a nuisance, one minute bragging and telling lies, and the next minute turning into a big frightened jelly. And now he thinks he's some sort of superhero or something. Look at him!"

The ghost was now pulling fearsome faces and swiping at the air with his short sword. "Just practising, mates!" he called cheerfully as he spotted them watching him.

"Idiot," muttered Tom, and looked away.

Bella was twisting some grass around her fingers. "You've got to think how he must feel, though," she said. "All those hundreds of years up on Hadrian's Wall, thinking about how he'd let his friends down and thinking about them all being killed, and not having any way to make up for it. And now, I suppose," she added thoughtfully, "he thinks he might get a second chance. You know, a chance to prove to himself that he's brave and useful. I really hope he does. Ahh! Just look at him. Isn't he lovely?"

Lovely was not the word Tom would have chosen to describe the ghost at that moment. With his bristly chin stuck out and his eyebrows knotted in a scowl, he was now throwing punches at a harmless little shrub and skipping about on his toes like a boxer.

Grandad, noticing the shrub shaking about, called, "Looks like the wind's getting up. Time we pressed on, eh?"

They all piled into the car and set off again, higher and higher into the mountains. The road grew steeper and narrower, the tall shoulder of the mountain looming on one side of them and a dizzy drop on the other. And it was not long before the ghost began fidgeting about on his cramped perch by the rear window. His sword kept prodding Tom in the back of the neck and Tom was getting fed up with it. "What's the matter with you now?" he hissed at last. "Not scared of heights as well, are you?"

"Listen, mate," said the ghost, craning round and moving his big knees so that he could see Tom's face. "I don't want to worry you or nothing, but I reckon we got trouble."

"Oh yeah?" sneered Tom. "That big bad caravan following us again, is it?"

"Don't" said Bella. "You're being mean."

The ghost looked confused. "Well, yeah, it is," he said. "But that i'n't what I mean. Look."

Tom and Bella turned to look out the rear window, straight through the front and back windows of the caravan at the steep road unwinding behind them. Close behind the caravan, a little blue car was following them. It was so close, in fact, that they could see the men in it quite clearly. There were four of them and they looked far too big for the little car, squeezed up close together, two in the front and two in the back. "Hey. They look like the men I saw at the petrol station," said Tom.

"They been behind us a long way now," said the ghost. "I don't like it. I don't like it at all."

Tom took a deep breath and blew it out impatiently. "There's bound to be people behind us, obviously," he said. "I mean, we were behind the people in front of us until it got steep and we couldn't keep up any more. But we weren't *following* them – not like how you mean."

But the ghost wasn't convinced. "There's four of them, right? And we got the Captain driving us. Now, I don't mean no disrespect to him, but his legs must be getting tired by now, and I reckon those four blokes could run that little car past us easy. But they haven't, have they? So, what I want to know is: why not?"

Tom stared at the ghost for a moment and then he slumped back down into his seat. "Stupid," he muttered.

"No falling out, you two," warned Grandma.

"Yes. Long way to fall, you know," joked Grandad, jerking his head towards the sheer drop on their left. They all laughed.

But now the road grew even steeper, and the car began to roar and shudder on the bends. They were losing speed, too; going so slowly now that they could almost count the blades of grass as they passed. The back of Grandad's neck was looking a bit red and hot, and everyone had stopped talking so that they could listen to the noises the engine was making as it struggled to haul the caravan behind it.

They made it around another bend, the car whining and chugging. "Are we alright?" asked Bella anxiously. She could see Auntie Eileen with eyes tightly shut rocking backwards and forwards, trying to help the car along.

"Should be alright," said Grandad hopefully, "as long as we keep going. Be at the top soon." He shifted the car into the lowest gear. "Mustn't let her stop, though. Never be able to set off again from a standing start, not at this gradient, not with the caravan. Dead weight, you see."

Bella peered across at the sheer drop on Tom's side of the car, and then put her hands over her eyes. "I don't like this," she whispered.

The ghost was just reaching out a grubby hand to pat her shoulder when suddenly, without warning, the little blue car behind them put on a burst of speed and roared past in a cloud of exhaust. Its driver and passengers were staring straight ahead; but as soon as they were past, they pulled in sharply in front of Grandad's car and dropped their speed to an absolute crawl, forcing Grandad to put on his brakes.

"Blithering idiots!" he muttered. "What do they think they're playing at?"

His car coughed and shuddered and tried valiantly to go on. But it had lost too much speed. The caravan plus the steep slope were just too much for it. It gave a last rattle as the engine stalled. And then there they were, stuck on the narrow mountain road with a sickening drop on one side of them and a wall of solid rock on the other.

chapter nine

In which we lose a hero.

Bella began to cry. Grandad mopped his face with a big red hanky. The ghost sat, grim and thoughtful, with his arm around Tom, while Auntie Eileen seemed to have gone to sleep. Either that or she'd fainted.

Only Grandma appeared happy. "Well?" she said to Grandad. "What did I tell you? There's a perfectly good tunnel through these mountains with a four lane motorway running through it. But oh no. *We* have to come over the top. You always have to be Scott of the bloomin Antarctic."

"Hannibal," said Grandad. "It was Hannibal who crossed the Alps. Didn't take his wife, though. Just elephants. Very sensible chap." He opened the car door and got out.

The little blue car had stopped too, a little further up the road. The four men had got out and were

leaning against it, smoking cigarettes and sneaking crafty looks in the direction of the Gypsy Belle.

Grandad patted the bonnet of his car to show it there were no hard feelings, and then stamped off round to the caravan to see what could be done. Tom and the ghost got out after him. The air felt strangely cold but very fresh, like the first morning of summer term, as Tom edged around the caravan, keeping a safe distance from the dangerous drop. He slipped his chilly hand into Grandad's large warm one. "Shall we turn around," he suggested, "and go back down to the tunnel like Grandma wanted?"

Grandad sighed. "Can't be done, I'm afraid," he said. "Road's too narrow. Don't like to sound gloomy, but we can't move forwards either. Too steep. Makes the 'van too heavy. And it's too risky to let her run back." He shook his head sadly. "No, Tommy Tucker. What we need's a bit of a push. Better go and ask those chappies up there, I suppose. All their fault in the first place."

He strode off up the road in his baggy shorts towards the four men. The ghost dropped his salute and turned frantically to Tom. "Stop him!" he shouted. "Can't he see? It's a set-up. It's a trick. They done it on purpose!"

Tom gazed uncertainly after Grandad, who had reached the men and seemed to be trying to explain what he wanted. But they were just staring back at him, insolently, tapping their cigarette ash into the breeze, making no move to help. The ghost gripped Tom's arm. "Tell him!" he urged desperately. "There's going to be trouble. Why's he think they've been following us like jackals and stopped us on this lonely bit of road?"

Grandad came stalking back, looking purple in the face and very angry.

"Tell him!" hissed the ghost.

"D'you think they're baddies, Grandad?" asked Tom.

"I don't doubt it for one minute," snapped Grandad. "The question is: what do we do now?"

"Permission to speak, sir?" said the ghost smartly. But, of course, Grandad didn't hear him. As far as he was concerned, the space the ghost stood in was just empty air.

"I want to volunteer to push, sir," the ghost persisted.

"Shut up," said Tom. "He can't hear you."

But Grandad was looking back over his shoulder. "Hello, hello," he said slowly. "Looks as though we're going to get some company."

Sure enough, the four men were sauntering towards them. The one in the front had his hands in his pockets. His cigarette hung from the corner of his mouth. The other three were showing their teeth, but they didn't look as though they were smiling. Nor did they look as though they were coming to help.

What should Tom and Grandad do? Leap into the car and lock the doors? Gather everyone together and run? Hope that some other car would come by? But the ghost had no doubts at all. He gave Tom a hefty shove towards the car. "Get in! Get in!" he yelled. "And get the Captain in! Tell him to try moving! I'll push! I'll push! Go on!"

Tom staggered and almost fell. "Quick, Grandad!" he squeaked. "Try and start her!"

Perhaps it was the urgency in Tom's voice, or the lack of any other plan, or the fact that the four men had taken their hands from their pockets and were closing in on them, that made Grandad jump into the car, start up the engine and slowly let the clutch out. Through the rear window Tom could see the ghost at the back of the caravan heaving and straining to take the weight. The four men broke into a run.

The engine whined and howled. The Roman soldier braced his legs and thrust with his massive shoulders, and noisily, inch by inch, the car and caravan began to move forward.

The engine was roaring and there was a burning smell, but slowly, steadily, they picked up speed. The four men threw themselves out of the way, scattering like skittles in a bowling alley. Tom and Bella looked back just in time to see them shouting angrily at each other and brushing down their sharp suits. And there was the ghost, staggering in the road, getting back his balance and, as the car and caravan pulled away, setting off hopelessly after them at a clumsy run. Then the road rounded a corner and flattened out and they were away, picking up speed, laughing and shouting and cheering.

"That got 'em!" shouted Tom. "That served them jolly well right."

"What's going to happen to those poor men, though?" said Auntie Eileen. "We nearly ran over them. Do you think they're alright?"

"Don't care," said Grandad grimly. "Highwaymen, if you ask me. And the faster we get away from them, the better."

"Pah!" laughed Grandma. "You watch too many cop shows on TV, that's *your* trouble."

They seemed to be on top of the whole world now, speeding along at a terrific pace with the Gypsy Belle bumping and swaying behind them. In front of them the road wove down, down, all the way to Italy. Grandad tapped out a tune on his steering wheel and began to sing:

"She'll be coming round the mountain when she comes.
She'll be coming round the mountain when she comes.
She'll be coming round the mountain,
Diddly diddly diddly..."

Auntie Eileen passed around the sweeties. They all settled back and began to smile again. All except Bella. Every time she blinked she could see the soldier's face as they left him behind. She could see the look in his eyes as they pulled away from him round that corner. And as they hurtled along on their way to Rome now without him, she could feel fat tears spilling over and wetting her cheeks.

chapter ten

A chapter of misunderstandings and fallings out.

They stopped for a late lunch in a small Italian town. Grandad and Bella went looking for a police station while Grandma, Auntie Eileen and Tom looked for toilets. Grandad and Bella were first to find what they were looking for.

The policeman sat behind a very large desk and was smoking a small cigar, which seemed to be stuck to his bottom lip. He smiled in a friendly way and amazed Bella by not dropping it. Then he slowly looked Grandad up and down, from his straw hat to his baggy shorts and sandals. "English?" he asked.

"Yes," said Grandad. "I mean, *si si*. Er…"

"It's ok, sir," said the policeman. "I speak perfect English. Please. Go ahead. What is your problem?"

"Puts me to shame," said Grandad. "Can't speak Italian. Well, just *spaghetti*. That's about it. Sorry."

"But he can speak French, can't you, Grandad?" said Bella, who felt she needed to stick up for him.

"Ah," said the policeman. "Perhaps you would rather we spoke in French?"

"No, no," said Grandad hurriedly. "No. English'll do. Thing is, I've come to report an attempted robbery. Or an attempted something. Not quite sure what." And he explained to the policeman what had happened: the blue car, the steep road, the four men who wouldn't help but approached threateningly. And the policeman listened to it all carefully, drawing little squiggles now and again on his notepad.

When Grandad had finished, the policeman sighed and pressed his lips together thoughtfully for a moment. "I am sorry," he said. "There is nothing I can

do. Even if I found the men, what would I arrest them for? Refusing to push your caravan? Walking towards you with their hands in their pockets?" He shook his head. "No, sir. I am sorry. Even though I suspect that this may have been the Somelli brothers. They are known to stop people in expensive cars and demand their watches, jewellery and money at gunpoint. But yours is a very ordinary car, you say. And you do not look – forgive me for saying so – you do not look as though you would be carrying great wealth."

"Don't mind you saying so at all," said Grandad. "But couldn't you at least arrest them for dangerous driving?"

The policeman smiled. "Sir, you have not yet been in Italy long enough to know what dangerous driving is."

"But," persisted Grandad. "What if they do it again? They may be following us."

Again, the policeman smiled. "They may indeed, sir, if – as you say – you are on your way to our capital city. For, as I am sure you know, sir, all roads lead to Rome."

Grandad and Bella walked back to the carpark where they had left the car and caravan. The sun shone hot, making the air in the middle distance shimmer and dance and the tall buildings throw cool, dark shadows in stripes across the pavement. "Never mind," said Grandad at last. "At least we know what they're called now. Dam' silly name though: *Smelly brothers*. You'd think they'd have done something about changing that, to *Smith* or something."

"Well, at least we'll smell them coming," said Bella; and that made Grandad laugh a lot, which cheered her up too.

But by the time they reached the caravan, she was finding it impossible to keep up a happy face. Every time she glanced around, half expecting to see the ghost, she saw only the solid shapes of real people, chattering and laughing and casting black shadows. And Tom looked just as sad as she felt.

The grownups were worried to see the children looking so miserable. "It's the shock," said Grandma to Grandad in a loud whisper, as they put up the awning at the campsite a few miles outside town. "It upset them, getting stuck on that mountain. It made them feel insecure. And you didn't help," she added sternly. "Panicking about those men and making a fuss to the police. The policeman probably thought you'd made it all up."

Grandma finally decided that the best way to make the children feel secure again was to get them to write a postcard each to Mum and Dad at home.

"Bloomin 'eck," grumbled Tom.

"Oh, come on," said Bella. "Let's do it. It'll make Grandma feel better if we do."

So they chose a postcard each from the camp shop. Tom's had a picture of a tower on it, leaning over to one side as if about to fall. He chewed his felt-tip pen for a minute or two and then wrote:

Dear Mum and dad
    Hop you are well it is very hot we are having
a grate time we haven't seen this tower.
    Love from Tom

Bella's card had a picture of a famous painting on it of ladies with fat bottoms.

Dear Mummy and Daddy, (she wrote)
    We are having a lovely time. We are eating a lot
of sweets. I am well, Grandma and Grandad are well.
    Auntie Eileen is well. I hope the cats are alright.
love from Bella xxxxxx
PS Tom is well

Grandma read them when they had finished. "Jolly good," she said. "Mummy and Daddy will be very pleased to get these." She gave them a couple of stamps and told them to take the cards down to the camp office where there was a post box.

When they got back, they found that Grandma, Grandad and Auntie Eileen had made friends with the English couple in the next caravan. They were all gathered in Grandad's awning, having a drink and saying what a nice awning it was. The children hung around for a while, being ignored. It was very hot, even though their pitch was under the shade of the camp's crooked, thirsty-looking trees, and they grumbled to each other for a while about how much nicer it would be if the campsite was near the seaside.

Then, "You shouldn't have let Grandad leave him behind," said Bella suddenly. "It wasn't fair. You promised to take him to Rome and now he's stranded and all because he wanted to help."

"It wasn't my fault," said Tom. "And anyway, who cares?" He was fed up with feeling hot and everybody getting at him.

"You should," said Bella.

Tom laughed to annoy her. "Why? Why should I?"

"Because you should!"

"*Because you should!*" he mimicked in a silly voice.

That was too much for Bella. She flew at him and grabbed a handful of his hair. He lashed out with both arms to try and make her let go. Her hot face was pressed against his ear and she was screaming, "You PIG! You PIG!" at the top of her voice.

A little crowd of children had gathered to watch and cheer by the time Grandad reached them. With a very loud, "THAT WILL DO!" he pulled Tom and Bella apart and marched them back to the caravan.

"Tut tut," said the lady from the caravan next door as they passed her in the awning. "I'm afraid you've got a handful there. Are they always so badly behaved?" Grandad bundled them inside and they didn't hear Grandma's reply.

"Well?" demanded Grandad when they were all three sitting down at the caravan table. The children glared at each other and said nothing.

"I don't expect you to tell me what you were fighting about," said Grandad, looking from one to the other of them sternly. "It's a hot day and we're all tired. But I DO expect you," he boomed suddenly, "to apologise for letting the side down and making such a silly scene."

"Sorry, Grandad."

"Sorry, Grandad."

"Righty-oh." He stood up and straightened his straw hat. "Now stay in here until you've made friends with each other. Have a little snooze if you're tired. I've got to get back to these dreadful new friends of your Grandma's." He left and closed the door gently behind him.

Tom had decided he was never speaking to Bella again. He knelt up on the seat to look at the grownups in the awning. They were standing about, chatting and sipping their drinks and occasionally laughing politely. The lady from the next caravan had earrings like great big plastic flowers which made Tom wonder whether she ever got attacked by bees. He hoped so. She was talking more loudly than anyone else. Auntie Eileen was smiling trying not to look bored. Grandad wasn't even trying.

It was her husband, though, who interested Tom, because he was almost completely bald and the sun had burnt the top of his head a dark angry red.

"Hey, come here a minute," said Tom to Bella. She clambered across and joined him by the window. He pointed at the man. "See him?" he said. "He looks like a tomato." They both giggled.

"Do you think he would grow some hair," said Bella, "if he watered his head?" They snorted with laughter. "Or," said Bella, "You know what? You know what Grandad puts on his garden to make things grow? Horse poo! He could put some horse poo on his head!" They fell against each other, laughing.

But now the man's face had turned as red as his head. He put down his glass, took his wife's arm, and they both stalked out of the awning and back to their own caravan.

Grandma burst in on Tom and Bella, and their laughter stopped.

"That was very rude!" she snapped. "We could hear every word you said. He was obviously very offended."

"Boring sort of chap," said Grandad, following her in, and looking quite cheerful. "Still, no call to be rude."

"You should try not to hurt other people's feelings, duckbods," said Auntie Eileen gently. "Nobody likes to be laughed at, unless they think it's funny too."

"Sorry," said Bella.

"Yes, sorry," said Tom meekly. But, surprisingly, no-one seemed to be really cross with them, and soon they were all busy getting tea ready.

Grandma had decided that, as they were in Italy, they should eat spaghetti. So they sat around the camp table, sucking the long, pale pasta off their forks as though eating worms. All except for Grandad. He prodded at his uncomfortably with his fork for a few minutes and then said he was sorry but, because of the hot weather, he wasn't very hungry.

A little later, the children bumped into him coming out of the camp shop eating an enormous toasted beef sandwich. When he saw them, he quickly swallowed his mouthful. Before they could speak, he said sternly, "Now then. I think it's time to find out what's been making you two behave like hooligans. Not like you at all. Glad it's all cooled down now."

They weren't sure whether he was talking about their tempers or his hot beef sandwich. But Bella felt it was time to come clean. Perhaps when he'd heard the whole story and how the ghost had saved them on the mountain, Grandad would drive back and help them find him.

Before Tom could stop her, she had begun: "We're sad because we've lost our ghost you see, Grandad. Tom found him on Hadrian's Wall and we were taking him to Rome because he was a Roman soldier, and he pushed the caravan when we were stuck but then we drove off so fast that he couldn't catch up with us. And now he's lost."

Grandad stared at her with his beef sandwich half way to his mouth. She did look sad. Her eyes were full of tears and she was twisting her fingers together anxiously. Then he looked at Tom, who was staring at the ground, tight-lipped and angry.

"Well," said Grandad after a moment. "No wonder. Very upsetting, losing a ghost. But I expect he's found some haunted house, eh? Gone to rattle his bones about and scare people, eh? Never mind." He patted Bella on the shoulder, pushed the rest of his sandwich into his mouth and hurried off to find Grandma.

"What did you go and say that for?" demanded Tom crossly when he'd gone. "He'll think we're stupid now. He'll think we made it up."

"I thought he might go back and find him," said Bella in a wobbly voice, and burst into tears.

Grandma appeared, hurrying towards them. She broke into a run when she saw that Bella was crying, and scooped her up into her arms.

Doesn't pick me up, thought Tom to himself bitterly. *Just because I don't cry. And anyway, he was my mate, not hers.*

But Grandma took hold of his hand and they all went back to the caravan. She sat down on the big comfortable seat and cuddled them both up to her. "You shouldn't play games that make you so upset," she scolded gently, rocking them back and forth. "You shouldn't go frightening yourselves. You know there are no such things as…"

At that moment there was a dreadful scream from the next door caravan and they all leapt up to the window to see what was wrong. They could see the bald man by his caravan door trying to calm his wife down. She was gasping and waving her hands about and one of her big plastic earrings had fallen off.

"A face! A face!" she screamed. "A horrible face! Staring in through the window! Take me home! I want to go home!"

It was only Tom and Bella who could see, lurking around the side of the Gypsy Belle, grinning in the gathering dark, the owner of the horrible face. A little more ragged, a little more dusty, but still unmistakably himself, the Roman ghost had somehow found them again.

chapter eleven

*In which we outrun the baddies again
and leave them behind. Or do we?*

There was a lot of fun and laughter at cocoa time, and suddenly the holiday was once again a big adventure.

"Funny coincidence, though," Grandad was saying. "Bella here talking about ghosts and then that dreadful Mrs Whatsername thinking she'd seen one." He shook his head and sipped his cocoa.

Meanwhile, the ghost, invisible again to everyone except Tom and Bella, was huddled in their corner with them, explaining how he'd found them. "I jumped in their car with them, see, when I knew I couldn't catch you up. And they all piled in, shouting at each other and waving their arms about, and shot off after you like a rock out of a catapult – car rattling and shaking like a seasick dog. Oh, sorry, mate," he said to Bella, who had pulled a disgusted face.

"Go on," urged Tom. "Then what?"

"I think," Grandad was saying, "that I'll probably write a letter to the Times about it. I shall call it, *A Strange Coincidence.*"

"I'm not surprised she was seeing things," said Grandma, "the way she got through my gin."

"Is that what happens when you drink gin?" asked Auntie Eileen with interest. She thought she had just seen Tom and Bella's mugs moving themselves about the table. "Perhaps I shouldn't have had any," she said.

"You was here, right?" the ghost was saying, moving Tom's mug along the table. "And we was here." He positioned Bella's a little way behind it. "I saw the back of you once or twice, disappearing around bends. And then we lost you." He absent-mindedly wiped his arm across the cocoa he'd spilt, but made no impression on it. "Anyway," he went on, "we come to this town, right? And I knew you'd be stopping somewhere soon because the Captain would need to rest his legs. So when they slowed down where two roads crossed, I got out."

"I was talking to this chappie in the showers," Grandad was saying. "Interesting sort. Travelled a lot."

"And?" said Grandma.

"Well," said Grandad, glancing at her nervously, "he told me that Italians don't just eat spaghetti on its own. They generally have something *on* it."

"Wasn't sure how I could find you," the ghost was saying. "So what d'you think I did?"

"Dunno," said Tom. "What?"

"I follered the signs, di'n't I?" He picked up the pencil and paper Grandad had been using to keep the scores for their game of Scrabble. (It made a change from Monopoly.) "This," he said. "I follered the signs what had this on." And very laboriously he drew:

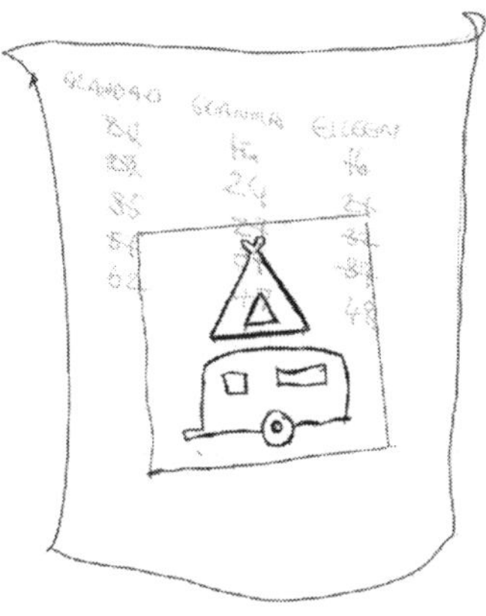

"See!" he said, leaning back and beaming with pride. That's called reading and writing. That's what *that*'s called."

Auntie Eileen, who had watched the pencil seem to draw all on its own, moaned softly. Grandma and Grandad, who had been too busy arguing about spaghetti to notice anything, looked across to see what was going on. "Look what Tom's done to my Scrabble score!" said Grandad indignantly. "He's drawn on it. I won that game and I got a jolly good score. I was going to keep that."

"Come on, Eileen," said Grandma briskly. "Time you were in bed."

The ghost watched the grownups with interest for a minute or two and then resumed his story. "I get here, right? And there's such a pigging lot of caravans – all look the same to me. So I go looking in all the windows. That's how I gave madam next door a fright. And good job, too. Moaning away, she was, about what horrible children you were. Well, I ain't having nobody talking like that about my mates. And you *are* my mates, aren't you?"

"S'pose so," said Tom, trying not to look too pleased. But Bella threw her arms around the ghost's mucky neck and hugged him tight. "I'm glad you're back," she said. And the ghost grinned, and blinked away the green tears that welled up in his shifty eyes.

*

The next morning, they were packed and ready to set off before the rest of the campsite began to stir. They hitched the caravan to the car and, as they set off down the driveway past the camp shop, Grandad began to sing his *Bella Marguerita* song that Bella always found so annoying.

And then he stopped mid-sing. Because there, parked by the campsite gates, was the little blue car. Inside it, through the steamed-up windows, they could see four men in suits, slumped asleep with newspapers over their faces.

"Well!" exploded Grandad. "The cheeky blighters! Lying in wait, eh? Right! I'll show 'em." He swung the car and caravan round into the main road and accelerated away with a great roaring of the engine, leaving a thick cloud of grey dust swirling behind them. The children peered behind excitedly to see whether the blue car was following them. But they could see nothing for the dust.

"I should just like to point out," said Grandma grimly, "that if it is the same car and if they are following us – though goodness knows why they'd want to – it might have been more sensible if we'd crept away quietly."

"Rubbish!" barked Grandad. "Show 'em you don't care. Stand up to 'em. That's the way to deal with their sort. Look 'em right in the eye."

"Yeah!" said the ghost excitedly (and mainly unheard), and almost fell off the back ledge and on to Auntie Eileen's knee with excitement.

"We're not exactly looking them in the eye at the moment, though, are we?" said Grandma. "We're more like running away from them at seventy miles an hour."

"Wonder what they're after," muttered Grandad, glancing in his mirror. There was still no sign of pursuit.

"Perhaps they just want to tell us something," suggested Auntie Eileen.

They were all starting to relax and Grandad had begun to sing again, when there was a sudden shout from Bella: "They're coming! Look! Quick, Grandad!"

And it was true. Although at the moment the car was no more than a blue speck, far, far behind them.

"They're not getting any bigger," said Tom after a while. "They're not catching up."

"No power in those little cars," said Grandad dismissively as they thundered on at breakneck speed down the hot dusty roads. Tall thin trees, pale houses, lonely-looking farm animals standing in little pools of their own shadow – all flashed by so quickly they scarcely saw them.

"Can't keep this pace up much longer," said Grandad eventually. "We'll have to stop for petrol soon and let the engine cool down a bit."

"Tell him to stop," said the ghost to Tom. "Tell him he's done amazing for a man of his age. I wish I had his legs. Tell him to stop and rest and I'll fight them off." His hand was straying restlessly to the hilt of his sword.

But Tom wasn't listening. "Hey," he said slowly. "I think we've lost them. They haven't come round the last bend yet and they weren't as far behind as that before."

"Right," said Grandad firmly. "Time for refreshments then. And we'll just have to trust to luck."

They pulled off the road on to a garage forecourt where there was also a café and ice-cream kiosk. A few minutes later they were all sitting on high stools at the café window, gazing cheerfully at the empty road. "Looks like we lost 'em," said Grandad cheerfully.

The ghost wasn't with them. He had taken it upon himself to guard the car, which they had left under the broad shade of a tree, its bonnet propped open to cool the engine.

"They probably over-heated," added Grandad. "Their car, I mean. Serve 'em right, too. Smelly Brothers, indeed."

Perhaps the family had all felt a little over-heated, too. But the ice-creams and chilled drinks soon set them right and, before long, they were ready to get back on with their journey. Tom and Bella returned to the car feeling happy and excited to be on the move again, and so it came as quite a shock to find the ghost looking grey-faced and anxious, all his old bravado gone.

"Oh here we go," said Tom. "What's up now?"

"I'm sorry, mate," said the ghost, "but I can't go with you. My luck's just turned bad. I'd be a danger to you. You'll have to leave me behind."

"Oh, for goodness sake!" said Tom.

"What's the matter?" Bella tried to take hold of the ghost's hand, but he drew it away uncomfortably. "What is it? Have you seen a magpie again?"

"Worse!" moaned the ghost. "Much worse."

"Come on, you two," said Grandad. "Don't stand there chattering. In you jump."

"It was horrible, mate, honest. It was this black cat. And it had a bird in its mouth."

"Ugh!" said Tom.

"Poor bird," said Bella.

"But not just any bird," whispered the ghost. "A hawk! A pigging hawk! And you know what that means."

"Let me guess," said Tom angrily, his face getting very red. "It means you're too scared to come with us. And after all that talk about never letting your mates down again. So now you're going to leave us just when we might be in danger. Just when we might need you. Some mate you are!" And he climbed into the car and slammed the door as hard as he could.

"Get in, Bella!" shouted Grandma. "What are you doing?"

"*Please* don't make us leave you behind again," said Bella to the ghost. "I can't bear it."

"You don't understand," whispered the ghost, miserably. "A cat with a hawk. It's an omen. It's a warning of danger. An ambush. I don't want to bring no trouble down on you…"

"*Please!*" begged Bella. She climbed into the car, leaving the door open for the ghost to follow. But it seemed he couldn't overcome his fear. Instead, he stared at her in anguish, wringing his hands, until

finally Grandma snapped at Bella to get the door shut, and they drove away.

It was worse this time, somehow – leaving him behind on purpose. And it had happened so quickly. Tom felt angry and Bella felt sad and they both felt hurt that he would just abandon them.

"Grandma," said Bella, after they'd travelled for a while in silence, "is it bad luck for a cat to catch a hawk?"

"Bad luck for the hawk," said Grandad. "Har! Har!"

"Not that I know of," said Grandma. "It's supposed to be bad luck to spill salt or break a mirror, and good luck to see a black cat. Or is that bad luck? But I've never heard of anything about hawks."

Something had brought them bad luck, however, because when they reached their next campsite that evening, they found it was full, and the man at the office had to turn them away.

Grandad switched on his torch and flicked through his book of campsites in the growing darkness.

"I knew we shouldn't have spent the afternoon sightseeing," said Grandma.

"My fault," said Grandad cheerfully. "And it looks as though we're miles from the next site, so I suggest we pitch camp over here in the woods. It won't matter. It's only for one night."

"What about toilets?" demanded Grandma.

"I'll dig you one," said Grandad. The children thought this sounded very interesting.

"What about the wild animals though, duckbods?" asked Auntie Eileen, looking around nervously.

"Well, I'm not digging them one," said Grandad. And they all laughed.

But it felt strange, setting up the caravan and awning in the eerie silence of the wood, with none of the bustle of a campsite but only the trees looking on, crowded around the clearing like the audience at a circus, waiting for something to happen.

Grandad dug a toilet – which turned out to be just a hole in the ground. And Tom went to the nearby stream and fetched water, which Grandma boiled for a long, long time and then dropped sterilizing tablets into, just to be on the safe side before she made the cocoa. They lit a small camp fire to keep wild animals away from Auntie Eileen, and sat around sleepily in the awning, sipping their bedtime drinks and listening to the rustling and twitching of the wood as it got ready for the night.

"I think this is great," said Tom to Bella. "If this is all the bad luck is, I don't call it bad luck at all. He was stupid not coming with us. He'd have really enjoyed this."

"He'd have stood on guard, wouldn't he?" said Bella wistfully. "And he'd have tried to look all important. Oh, why did he have to be so silly? And after going to all that trouble to find us again, too."

"What's that?" said Auntie Eileen suddenly. They all turned to look at her. "Sssshhhh!" she said. "Listen!"

They strained their ears to hear past the crackling of the fire and the creaking of the night-time insects.

"There!" said Auntie Eileen. There was a soft rustle and snap that might have been stealthy footsteps somewhere beyond their circle of light. They held their breaths and strained their ears and eyes into the darkness. And it came again, louder this time, nearer. Grandad half rose from his chair.

"Probably just a fox," said Grandma hopefully. Her voice sounded brisk and loud in the waiting silence. "SSSSHHHHHHHH!" they all said.

Again the sounds came, much closer now, as though whatever was coming was no longer taking care to be quiet.

"A nature warden, probably," said Grandad, sounding unconvinced and reaching for his stick. "Or yes, maybe a fox."

But it was neither a nature warden nor a fox who stepped suddenly into the ring of firelight. It was someone they had seen before. He wore a sharp suit and a black moustache. He grinned an evil grin as his three brothers stepped out of the darkness behind him. "So," he said. "This time we do a business. You will give me alla your moneys. Alla your moneys what is so much it afalls offa the table. Everything. And then there willa be no trouble."

One of the men behind him leaned forward and whispered something in his ear. "And," added the man with black moustache, "alla your English stamps. For my brother."

And with that, he took out of his pocket an ugly-looking pistol and pointed it at the horrified family in the awning.

chapter twelve

*A chapter of heroes and villains,
in which there is a big fight.*

Grandma was the first to speak. "Well," she said to Grandad, "here's your big chance to look them in the eye. What are you waiting for?"

Grandad cleared his throat and then, lowering his eyebrows in a ferocious frown, he fixed the armed robber with a hard, unblinking stare. The robber looked puzzled for a moment, but then grew angry. "What you standa there for, looking like-a the goldfish?" he demanded. "Give me your money! *Pronto!*"

"His name's not Pronto, duckbods," said Auntie Eileen helpfully. "It's…"

"SILENCE!" bawled the robber. He turned his gun on Auntie Eileen, "You first. Show me what you got inna the bag."

Auntie Eileen tried to explain that she didn't have any foreign money because it didn't have a picture of the Queen on it. But he made her empty her bag and out fell wine gums, barley sugars, smarties, mint rock, scattering all over the table and spilling to the ground. As she shook the bag to make sure it was completely empty, a couple more fell out, unrecognisable and covered in fluff. Out, too, fluttered the letter Auntie Eileen had received at the last campsite from her daughter in England. The robber pounced on it eagerly and tore the stamp from the envelope. "I will have this," he said, and passed it back to the brother who'd whispered in his ear.

Auntie Eileen tried to draw all the robbers' attention to what a nice picture of the Queen there was on the stamp. But the one with the gun was getting more and more angry. "Now!" he shouted at Grandad. "All your money! Quick! I know you have money here, more money than the bank. I hear you talking. Thousands and thousands of money, all over the table. You pretend to be ordinary man but you own many, many hotels." He tapped the side of his nose. "I know it. You think I am stupid. But I am not stupid."

"Actually, you are, a bit stupid," said Tom. "That wasn't real money we were talking about. It was…"

"SILENCE!" the robber roared, and turned to point his gun at Tom.

"Oh, don't do that, duckbods," said Auntie Eileen anxiously. "I'm sure you're not bad really. I expect it's just that your mummy didn't love you."

"Not surprised," muttered Grandad.

But this was too much for the robber. "You leave my mamma outa this!" he cried. And, with a terrific kick, he sent the camp table flying and the sweets scattering in the air, hitting the caravan side like bullets. "Now!" he panted. "All-a that money! Quick!" He levelled the gun at Grandad again and his three brothers stepped forward threateningly. The firelight set their shadows jumping and lit their faces with an evil reddish light that drove their eyes deep into their sockets. Bella shivered and hung on to Tom's arm. She could hear the tiny whisper of Grandad's wrist-watch ticking, and felt her heart beating almost as fast.

Grandma broke the silence. "Well, I think we've more or less proved that staring at them doesn't do any good," she snapped. "Better give them what they want. Get your money belt off, Grandad."

Grandad sighed and untucked his shirt. Strapped around his middle, over his vest, was a thick leather belt with pockets in it. This was where he tucked the holiday money away each time he drew some out. He unbuckled it now and slung it at the robber's feet. "Here. Take it, you swine!" he said.

The robber rifled through it with greedy fingers and then threw it angrily on the ground. "This is nothing! Give me your thousands and thousands! Now!"

"We were talking about Monopoly money, you idiot," said Tom, bravely. The robber swung round again to point his gun at the children.

"Now look here!" said Grandad indignantly, stepping forward.

"QUIET!" bawled the robber. "Or I shoot." He waggled the gun like a cross finger at Tom and Bella. "So now you show me *your* moneys."

"Bloomin 'eck," said Tom. "That's not fair. I've saved my pocket money up all year for this." He took his plastic wallet out of his jeans pocket and held it for a moment in his hand. He was thinking of all the times he'd cleaned Mum and Dad's car, and set the table, and run down to the shop, all to earn this holiday spending money. And now this stupid man was going to take it. It would mean no ice creams, no souvenirs, no presents to take back home for Mum and Dad.

But the robber had no thought for things like that. He snatched the wallet from Tom's hand and then grabbed Bella's blue knitted purse which she was holding out to him.

"You can have the money, but please can I have my purse back?" said Bella in a small voice. "I knitted it myself." But the robber either didn't hear or didn't care, because having emptied out the coins into the palm of his hand, he tossed the purse over his shoulder onto the campfire, where it scorched and shrank and disappeared into the flames.

"You rotten bounder!" gasped Grandad. But the robber wasn't listening. He'd passed the money to his brothers to share out and was now busy forcing Grandma to open up her handbag. It was a big heavy one with metal-bound edges, especially useful for carrying her books about. There was a gleam in her eye as she allowed the robber to dip his hand inside. And then, with a loud, "GOT YOU!" she snapped it closed on his fingers.

He staggered back, howling, and his brothers ran forward to catch him just in time to prevent him from falling with his bottom in the fire. All the family sniggered with delight, except for Auntie Eileen, who was worried he might have burnt his bum.

But it was his pride that had suffered most, and of course this made him furious. "You thinka that's funny?" he shouted. "Well, I teacha you a lesson you don't forget. You tell me where you hide your thousands right away, *now*, or I shoota your caravan full of holes!"

"No!!" they all cried. But he levelled his gun at the side of the Gypsy Belle, grinning and taking careful aim. Bella closed her eyes and Auntie Eileen stopped, horrified, in the middle of picking up her sweets. Grandad was calculating the distance between himself and the gun and wondering whether he could knock it aside, when he saw a strange thing happen.

Instead of pulling the trigger, the robber seemed to jerk up into the air, the gun spinning from his hand as he flew several meters backwards smack into the middle of his brothers, knocking them over like a football hitting milkbottles.

"What the…?" began Grandad. But there was no time for puzzlement. The robbers were picking themselves up and glaring fiercely about them. Grandad sprinted for the gun, but one of the robbers tripped him up before he got there. They grappled together on the ground for a moment until the robber suddenly slumped unconscious. "But I never even…" squeaked Grandad, turning to see the chief robber staggering under a rain of invisible blows, taking one too many steps backwards, stumbling, and falling into the newly-dug toilet, which – unfortunately for him – all the family had taken it in turns to try out earlier. Two of his brothers were out cold on the ground, but one – the stamp collector – was still on his feet and trying to race Grandad to the fallen gun, when a short piece of fallen branch rose into the air and came down with a thump on the robber's head. His eyes rolled up to look at the night sky, his knees buckled, and he flopped, face-down, on the grass.

Grandad reached the gun and looked around, panting, for someone to point it at. But all the Somelli Brothers lay around him, dazed or unconscious – one rather more smelly now than the others. "Crikey," said Grandad in a small voice.

Of course, he and Grandma and Auntie Eileen hadn't seen what Tom and Bella had seen. They hadn't seen the Roman ghost creep into the firelight, put his finger to his lips and wink at them. They hadn't seen him pick up the chief robber, kick away his gun, throw him to the ground, and then set about his brothers with his fists. It had all happened so quickly that the grownups were not quite sure *what* they had seen. Grandma and Auntie Eileen had certainly seen Grandad diving about a lot and tussling with one of the robbers, and they concluded that he must have won the fight all by himself, single-handed. They were still looking at him with admiration as he asked Tom to go and get the tow rope from the boot of the car.

Tom came running back with it. "Er…right," said Grandad, still looking rather stunned. He peered at the gun closely and then put it down carefully on the grass. "Turns out it's not a real one," he said. "But still – best not point it at anyone." He took the rope from Tom. "Well done, Tommy Tucker."

Tom winked at the ghost and the ghost winked back. Bella was hugging his big hairy leg and telling him how pleased she was that he'd decided to follow them after all.

"I saw they was still follering you," said the ghost gruffly. "What else could I do? I grabbed a ride on their roof, and then…well, here I am."

"Oh, and you are so brave!" said Bella. The ghost's nostrils flared and he glowed green with pride.

Grandma and Grandad had hauled all the robbers into a heap and tied them together with the rope. The brothers were a sorry sight, bruised and battered, their smart suits all rumpled. One of them began to moan. Grandma brought her handbag down sharply on his head and he fell quiet again.

"Sorry I went on that time about you winning at Monopoly, Grandad," said Tom. "If I hadn't done that…"

"Don't worry," said Grandad. "Apology accepted."

Grandma was beaming at Grandad. Her face was quite pink. "Do you know," she said, "that was the bravest thing I've ever seen. Fighting all those robbers single-handed and beating them. You really are my hero." And she flung her arms around Grandad's neck and hugged him so hard that he could barely get his breath. "You were so masterful," she said.

"Was I?" wheezed Grandad. "I mean," he added, clearing his throat and speaking in a deeper voice, "I mean, I was. Yes. No doubt about it." He swept one last bewildered glance around the clearing. "Suppose it must've been me," he muttered to himself. "Heat of the moment and all that."

Auntie Eileen was still picking up her sweets. "Do you think I ought to put a few in their pockets for when they wake up?"

"No," said Grandad masterfully. "And that reminds me." He bent down and turned out the robbers' pockets until he had all the stolen money back. Auntie Eileen insisted, though, that they not take back the stamp.

"Let him keep it, duckbods," she said. "My Ron used to collect stamps. I remember," she added wistfully, "how cross he used to get when I hid them or threw them away."

"So," said Grandma to Grandad, "what do we do now?"

"Well," said Grandad in a deep voice, "I suggest we take them to the nearest police station."

And so that's what they did. The Somelli Brothers had a very uncomfortable journey, trussed together and jolted about in the caravan. When Grandad opened the door to haul them out at the police station, he found that a cupboard door had sprung open on the way and a bottle of tomato sauce had emptied itself all over the robbers' heads. They did look very silly as the police officers hauled them away to the cells, still tied together, stumbling with their eight legs like a big stupid spider.

It was past midnight now, and everyone was very tired. The police officers, when they had finished shaking Grandad's hand and patting him on the back, offered to let them pitch camp for the rest of the night in the police station garden. As the Police Chief helped them guide the caravan in, she told them, beaming, that if they left her their address in England, she would send them the reward. The Italian police had been looking for the Somelli Brothers for a very long time.

Later, as they were getting the sleeping bags out, Grandma announced that there would be more room for the children to sleep soundly tonight if she joined Grandad in the awning. Of course, this meant that the ghost had a bit more room, too. He stretched out on the big bed beside Auntie Eileen, who was already sound asleep.

"You should have the reward really," Bella whispered across to him before she closed her eyes.

"No, mate," he said gruffly. "There i'n't nothing else what I could ask for. I got some good mates and I got my pride back, like. That's all I want. That's all I ever wanted."

And Bella thought for a moment that she glimpsed the corner of the pillow through the dark shadow where the ghost's shoulder should be. How strange! He hadn't appeared transparent to her since that first day she'd seen him, back at home. But she was too tired to puzzle over it, and in a few seconds she was so fast asleep that she couldn't even hear Grandad snoring loudly and contentedly in the awning.

chapter twelve-and-a-half

In which we finally reach Rome.

Next morning at breakfast, while everyone munched their rolls and jam, Grandad was treated to big plateful of eggs, bacon, mushrooms, tomatoes and fried bread. "He still has a lot of driving to do," Grandma explained. "He has to keep his strength up." The ghost, meanwhile, was lounging happily against the wardrobe door, watching them.

"We'll be in Rome today, won't we, Grandad?" said Tom.

"About lunchtime," said Grandad. "Right on schedule."

Tom grinned at the ghost and gave him a thumbs up sign.

"I bet you're tired after all that fighting, aren't you, duckbod?" said Auntie Eileen to Grandad. "Would you like my toast, look?"

"No," said Grandad. "But thank you all the same. Strange thing," he went on. "I'll never really know how I sorted those villains out. It was four against one, you know."

"Instinct," said Grandma. "I expect it all just came back to you, from your time in the army."

"Must've done," said Grandad.

Bella nudged Tom and they both chuckled.

"No tittering at the table!" boomed Grandma. "Time to get packed up and off. Right, Grandad?"

"Oh, absolutely," said Grandad, wiping his plate with the fried bread and stuffing the last of it in his mouth.

They set off. The road was lined either side with tall trees the shape of spears. Here and there a house sat and baked in the sunshine, and the heat shimmered on the road like pools of water that turned mysteriously back to tarmac as they came closer. All the car windows were open, and the air that rushed in was almost as warm as the blast from a hair dryer.

This was the bright sun and the lazy heat that the ghost must remember from all those hundreds of years ago when he was alive and growing up, thought Bella. So how ever had he been able to bear it: all those centuries up there in the north on the Wall, where even in summer the wind blew so cold?

Tom sat between the ghost's knees, just as he had on that first car journey together. But this time, at last, the soldier seemed calm and relaxed. He no longer shook with fear to see the oncoming traffic. And he seemed somehow to take up less room than he used to. Perhaps, thought Tom, it was because at last he was almost home.

"Here we are!" cried Grandad, as the trees on either side gave way to tall buildings and the road became much more busy with traffic. Shoppers and tourists crowded the pavement and spilled over into the road where they were blared at by car horns. Caught in the stream of vehicles, the car and caravan inched along, giving the children plenty of time to look out of the windows and exclaim.

"Whoa!" shouted Tom. "Look at those ruins!" He could see archways and tall pillars of pale marble, half tumbled as though a giant baby had knocked over its building blocks.

"And look at that!" said Bella, as a huge round building made of arches came into view. Traffic was whizzing around it, using it as a giant roundabout. "What's that?"

"It's the Coliseum," said Grandma. "Where the gladiators used to fight. And people had to fight wild animals."

"Oh dear," said Auntie Eileen, in a small voice.

"Rome at last," said Bella. "Yippee!"

And she bounced up and down on the back seat with excitement. But when she turned to give the ghost a reassuring pat on the knee, she drew in her breath, horrified. "Tom! Look!" she said. "Look what's happening to him!"

Tom looked down and saw that Bella's hand had passed right through the ghost's leg and was patting instead the warm leather of the car seat. He twisted round to get a better look. There was the ghost still, silhouetted against the car window, wearing an unfamiliar but very happy smile. And through him, beyond him, Tom could see the crowded streets of Rome, the traffic, the tourists, the tall sunlit buildings.

"He's going!" he whispered to Bella. "He's fading away!"

"Oh no!" Bella whispered back. "Not yet. Please. Don't go. Not just like that." She tried to take the ghost's hand, but there was nothing solid there, only a picture on the air, like breath on a glass.

"First thing I'm going to do," said Grandad happily, "once we get parked, is to take you all for a real Italian spaghetti meal."

"Lovely!" said Auntie Eileen.

Grandma said nothing.

"Alright, kiddies?" Grandad called back over his shoulder.

There was no answer.

Auntie Eileen reached across and patted Tom's hand. "Grandad says are you alright, duckbods."

"Oh," said Tom quietly. "Yes. Thank you."

But he didn't feel alright at all. His friend was disappearing even as he looked at him, and there was nothing he could do to make him stay.

"Auntie Eileen leaned forward and whispered in Grandma's ear. "They don't look very well to me, duckybods. I think it might be the heat."

"Stop the car, Grandad," ordered Grandma promptly.

"*What??*" said Grandad, horrified. "*Here?*" They were surrounded by five lanes of crazily speeding traffic.

"Here," said Grandma. "At once, please."

Grandad stopped.

Grandma got out and opened the children's door. Horns blared. Whistles blew. Cars whizzed by and roared around them. The city was all a-rumble with noise, and the heat beat down on the stones and the road. Grandma pulled Tom and Bella round into the shade of the caravan. "Take some deep breaths," she ordered. The air smelt of hot metal and exhaust fumes. She pointed at the Coliseum. "Just look at that," she said. "Still standing. And it's been here since Roman times. Isn't it marvellous?"

Out of the open car door something drifted like a winter's breath on the air. A small breeze caught it and blew it gently upwards, past the heat haze shimmering on the car roofs, up towards the blue sky, above all the noise and roar, until it was lost in the brightness of the sunshine.

"I'll always miss him," said Bella quietly that evening as they sat in the restaurant, winding spaghetti carbonara around their forks. "But he's happy now though. That's the main thing."

"Yeah," said Tom with his mouth full. "But you know what? I never actually got to have a go with his sword."

Auntie Eileen leaned past Grandma and Grandad, who were smiling happily together, and dropped a little package on to Bella's knee. "It's nothing really, duckbods," she said. "Just something I found in the gift shop. I thought you might like it. To remind you."

Bella tore off the wrapping paper and out fell a little brown leather purse, stitched around with red. And on it, drawn in red and gold, was a picture of a Roman soldier leaning on his sword and smiling.

Bella and Tom stared at it, and then up at Auntie Eileen, their mouths open in surprise. But Auntie Eileen just smiled back at them mischieviously, and winked.

I suppose you're wondering why this was called Chapter Twelve-and-a-half. Well, for one thing, it's not very long. And, for another, I don't think the ghost would have liked to be in a story with *thirteen* chapters. Do you?

For exclusive discounts on Matador titles,
sign up to our occasional newsletter at
troubador.co.uk/bookshop